A SIMPLE CASE OF ANGELS

A SIMPLE CASE
OF ANGELS

✳

CAROLINE ADDERSON

Groundwood Books / House of Anansi Press
Toronto Berkeley

Groundwood Books / House of Anansi Press
110 Spadina Avenue, Suite 801, Toronto, Ontario M5V 2K4
or c/o Publishers Group West
1700 Fourth Street, Berkeley, CA 94710

We acknowledge for their financial support of our publishing program the
Canada Council for the Arts, the Government of Canada through the Canada
Book Fund (CBF) and the Ontario Arts Council.

Canada Council   Conseil des Arts
for the Arts   du Canada

ONTARIO ARTS COUNCIL
CONSEIL DES ARTS DE L'ONTARIO

Library and Archives Canada Cataloguing in Publication
Adderson, Caroline, author
A simple case of angels / by Caroline Adderson.

Issued in print and electronic formats.
ISBN 978-1-55498-428-2 (bound).—ISBN 978-1-55498-429-9 (pbk.).—
ISBN 978-1-55498-430-5 (html)
1. Dogs—Juvenile fiction. I. Title.

PS8551.D3267S54 2014   jC813'.54   C2014-900972-0
                                       C2014-900973-9

Cover illustration by Nina Cuneo
Design by Michael Solomon

Printed and bound in Canada

MIX
Paper from
responsible sources
FSC® C016245
www.fsc.org

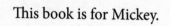

This book is for Mickey.

Thank you to Shelley, Sheila and Jackie — the three angels who helped this book come to be.

1

WHAT MUST have happened was this. Sometime during summer holidays, the ground the school stood on, the playground surrounding it, and the soccer field, too — *t i l t e d.*

Not a lot. Just enough that the queen's picture in the front entrance of Queen Elizabeth Elementary School hung crookedly, the crown askew on Her Majesty's head. Just enough, too, that in September, when most of last year's grade fours were moving to their new grade-five classroom, someone dropped a water bottle and it rolled the entire unscuffed summer-polished length of the hall.

Nicola Bream's friend Mackenzie Stewart changed classes. Nicola hadn't seen her for two months because the Stewarts spent every summer at their cottage.

"See you at recess!" Mackenzie called to Nicola.

"I got something!" Nicola called back. "You'll be really surprised! I can't wait to show you!"

Nicola stayed in her old desk in her old classroom with her old teacher, Ms. Phibbs, and a half-dozen other kids from last year. Mostly boys, some of them awful, like Gavin Heinrichs. Soon the new grade fives joined them, kids who had changed schools.

Then, to Nicola's dismay, the rest of the desks filled up with little children. Last year's grade threes.

A split class!

At recess Nicola couldn't find Mackenzie. When she couldn't find her at lunch, she sat alone at a picnic table drawing pictures of her dog, June Bug.

June Bug was the surprise she'd mentioned to Mackenzie.

Every time Nicola set down a pencil crayon — white, black, white — it rolled off the end of the picnic table and onto the ground.

Because the picnic table, like the picture of the queen and the school named after the queen, had tilted.

✳

Something else was different that fall. There were hardly any birds. Though it was too early for them to migrate south for the winter, they seemed to be gone already, taking with them their cheerful songs. The few times Nicola spotted a lone sparrow sitting tongue-tied in a bush with its feathers all puffed up, it always looked in a very bad mood.

After just a week of grade five, Nicola could say the same about Ms. Phibbs. Last year she'd been so nice, but this year she was short-tempered and counted spelling.

And her brothers — awful! Nicola fought with them more and more, mostly over June Bug. Between Mackenzie acting like she didn't even know Nicola now, and Ms. Phibbs taking off so many marks because Nicola could never sort out *there* from *their* and *they're*, and her brothers being so mean, life would have been unbearable. If not for June Bug.

June Bug was still a puppy, but so smart. She understood words and did tricks and even made up her own games. Like grabbing hold of the end of the toilet-paper roll and running through the house unspooling it. When the Breams moved the toilet paper onto the windowsill, out of reach, June Bug invented a new game. She figured out how to step on the little pedal on the bathroom wastebasket to make the lid flip up. Then she would dig inside and throw the garbage around. All kinds of awful, embarrassing stuff ended up all over the floor, like snotty tissues and cotton swabs all yellow with earwax.

After that the Breams kept the bathroom door closed.

The second week of school, Nicola's big brother did something he'd never done before. Jared brought home a girl. Her name was Julie Walters-Chen, and she smelled of shampoo and wore ironed jeans.

Clothes-and-hair girls were not interesting to Nicola. Every morning she put on whatever she found in her dresser. Her hair hung in a messy braid down her back. Her mother, Mina, complained it looked like an old rope that had been enthusiastically chewed. Which it had.

But Jared was interested in Julie Walters-Chen. Nicola could tell by the way he twitched around her, like his arms and legs were attached to strings. Also he blushed a lot, which masked his pimples.

Jared and Julie went straight to his room to listen to music.

"Leave the door open," Mina called. She was working from home that day.

To Nicola, Mina said, "I don't want Jared closing himself in there with a girl."

"Right," Nicola said.

She checked Jared's door, then tiptoed back to the den to report to her mother that it was hardly even open, only a crack.

June Bug, meanwhile, had pulled one of Nicola's mother's bras out of the laundry hamper and was trotting down the hall with it. The little dog wanted someone to chase her.

Hearing voices in Jared's room, June Bug burst in.

As soon as she saw Julie, June Bug jumped up on the bed and tried to kiss her. Which was when Jared, his back to Julie, turned on the music.

Whenever June Bug heard Jared's rap, she went berserk. She barked at the vacuum the same way, and the hairdryer. When anything electric made a noise, June Bug had to make a louder noise.

One moment Julie Walters-Chen was sitting on the edge of Jared's bed smoothing her long, perfect hair. The next, a dirty bra lay in her lap and a strange dog was licking her face. Then came the crazy barking.

It was too much. Shrieking and flapping her hands in fright, Julie bolted from Jared's bedroom and right out of the house.

"Julie!" Jared called after her. "Come back!"

She didn't.

Jared swung around to face Nicola. "Either that dog goes or I do!" He pointed at little June Bug wagging at his feet.

And right then, right as he shouted that? June Bug peed on the floor.

Nicola thought that showed how smart her dog was.

Jared said go, so she went.

2

————

OTHER STRANGE things happened, too. During the first few weeks of school not one but *several* kids fell off the playground equipment at Queen Elizabeth Elementary. Nicola, stuck inside during recess correcting her spelling, happened to see some of these falls.

Nicola didn't mind staying in. There was nothing to do at recess now anyway.

Last year Nicola and Mackenzie Stewart had made up games, like ABC Gum World. They saved their Already Been Chewed gum and brought it to school in baggies. At recess and lunch they snuck away to a private corner of the schoolyard behind a smooth-barked tree. There they rechewed the gum to soften it, then shaped it into animals and people. They stuck their creations on the tree — a whole pink and purple Already Been Chewed Gum World they invented stories about.

Nicola remembered this while gazing out the classroom window and not correcting her spelling. The window looked over the playground. Lost in thought, she barely noticed from the corner of her eye what fell.

A kid in a green jacket. He'd climbed all the way to the top of the jungle gym, then tried to stand. Arms windmilling, he plunged.

A playground monitor rushed over to check on the fallen boy. At just that moment, a kid at the top of the slide lost his balance, too, and fell. Then another.

It was so strange, children dropping like apples out of a tree. Nicola almost laughed.

The next day the school board sent out an inspector who wound every fun thing in the playground with yellow tape. The principal, Mrs. Dicky, announced over the intercom that there had been some seismic activity in the area.

"What's that?" asked Lindsay Feeler, a new girl with short brown hair and pink-framed glasses who sat next to Nicola this year instead of Mackenzie.

Ms. Phibbs shushed her. Last year Ms. Phibbs had welcomed questions that deepened their understanding of the world. This year she said they talked too much.

Mrs. Dicky declared the playground closed until further notice.

✳

Jared, of course, blamed June Bug for driving away Julie Walters-Chen. He hated June Bug for it. But when he came in the door, June Bug still rushed to greet him and wag all around him.

"Go to hell," Jared told the little dog.

"You swore," Nicola said.

"It's not a swear. It's a place. And that's where that dog is going."

Her little brother, Jackson, who was in kindergarten, imitated everything Jared said and did. He would chant, "Go to hell! Go to hell!" to the poor little dog, who wagged excitedly, not realizing he was saying something mean.

When their father, Terence, heard Jackson say, "Go to hell," and found out that Jared had taught him, he lost his temper, which didn't happen very often.

"You watch your language, young man!" he yelled at Jared, who stormed off to his room and slammed the door. Jackson got a time-out, too, for saying a bad word.

"June Bug should get a time-out!" he wailed. "She ate my Ferrari!"

"She ate it?"

"The wheels!" He ran and got it, another disabled Matchbox car.

Terence said, "Time out, June Bug! Nicola, put her in your room. You, too, Jackson! Go to your room!"

Nicola went with June Bug. Together they lay on the bed. June Bug chewed Nicola's long braid, while Jackson tantrummed through the wall. He was still bawling when their mother came home from work.

Over Jackson's wails, Nicola heard Mina ask Terence what had happened.

She heard her father's reply. His exact words. They froze her blood.

"It's not working out with that dog."

3

———

AT THE PICNIC table, under the trees empty of birds, Nicola sat drawing. Lindsay Feeler joined her. She didn't ask if Nicola minded. Maybe she thought that since their desks were side by side, she could sit with her whenever she wanted.

"I like drawing, too," Lindsay said, pushing up her pink-framed glasses.

She opened a huge case of gel pens — 100, the label read — and spread her drawings around. Nicola couldn't help seeing them, though she kept her eyes on her own paper.

Lindsay's drawings were of girls in long white dresses standing against flowery backgrounds. The way Lindsay arranged them on the picnic table made Nicola feel surrounded by the same kind of girls that Mackenzie Stewart now spent every recess and lunch with, trading jewelry and hair thingies on the front steps of the school.

Lindsay Feeler and Nicola Bream drew in silence. Every time Nicola set down her pencil crayon, it rolled off the table and onto the ground. Every time, Lindsay bent to retrieve it, then placed it beside her huge gel pen case so it wouldn't roll away again.

Finally, Lindsay spoke. "That's a really cute dog."

"She's my dog and she's in so much trouble," Nicola said.

"What trouble?"

"It would take me a week to explain. Now they're talking about getting rid of her. And not only that. I'm afraid she'll go to hell!"

Nicola felt the sting of tears. She blotted her eyes on her sleeve.

Somehow these two things got mixed together in Nicola's mind — the fear of losing her dog and her fears for her dog. Because if June Bug was sent away, if she didn't have Nicola to help her behave, she would become a force of destruction. She really would.

Without Nicola, she'd end up in a time-out for the rest of her life.

Wouldn't that be the same as hell?

※

That night, when Mina came into her room to ask why she was so quiet at dinner, Nicola hid her face in her pillow.

"You must be pretty disappointed not to be in the same class as Mackenzie this year," Mina said.

"I don't care."

"At least you have Ms. Phibbs again."

Nicola let out a loud, watery sniff.

"Well, please tell me if I can help," Mina said.

Nicola lifted her face out of the pillow and said goodnight.

After Mina left, Nicola cried herself to sleep.

4

"YOU SHOULD take your dog to church," Lindsay Feeler whispered to Nicola during gym when they were both dead.

First Nicola got killed because she hated Murder Ball so much. While everyone was running amok, she stood with her eyes squeezed shut, waiting for the death blow. Then she could sit down on the floor and forget about getting hit.

Last year they never played Murder Ball. They did proper things in gym class, like basketball and gymnastics. Things that didn't hurt.

As soon as Nicola got murdered, Lindsay came and stood beside her. Anyone not moving was doomed.

Smack! The ball struck her between the shoulder blades. She grunted and sank down next to Nicola.

"Confess for your dog," she whispered. "Then she won't go to hell."

"Really?" Nicola asked.

"I think so," Lindsay said. "When you confess, it's like erasing every bad thing you've done."

All around them, their classmates were stampeding from one corner of the gym to the other, screaming and yelling. Ms. Phibbs seemed to have left.

"Do you go to church?" Nicola asked.

"No," said Lindsay, "but I know a bit about it from the manager in my apartment building. He works in a church near where I live. I'll take you there. You can confess for June Bug."

"When?" Nicola asked.

Lindsay took a paper out of her back pocket and unfolded it. On it were dates and times in a kid's printing.

"Oh, look," she said. "You could go this Saturday."

✳

"It's nice that you've made a new friend," Mina told Nicola on Saturday morning as she was straightening the pictures on the living-room walls. She straightened them every few days, but they always ended up crooked again.

"She's not a friend," Nicola said. "She's the girl I sit beside."

Lindsay Feeler was hurrying up the walk now. June Bug, standing on the back of the couch watching out the window, started beating her stubby tail at the sight of a visitor.

"Oh," Lindsay cried when Nicola opened the door.

"Is that June Bug? She looks exactly like your drawing!"

Lindsay crouched to pat the wagging dog.

"I just want to call your mother," Mina said. "To make sure that Nicola is invited."

"My mom isn't home. She works on Saturday. She's a florist."

Mina glanced at Nicola. "I'm afraid I'm not comfortable with you girls being without adult supervision."

"Oh, I'm without it all the time. The apartment manager keeps an eye on me. And my mom's shop is nearby. She's the cutest dog I've ever seen!"

June Bug seemed to like Lindsay, so much that Nicola should have warned her. If June Bug really, really liked someone, she would —

"Ouch!" Lindsay straightened with her hand over her nose.

"No, June Bug!" Mina and Nicola scolded.

"Anyway, we're not going to my house," Lindsay said, dabbing at her nose to see if it was bleeding. "Didn't Nicola tell you? We're going to a wedding."

"We are?" Nicola said.

"Yes, and we'd better hurry because it starts at eleven. I want to get there before the bride."

Somehow Lindsay managed to convince Mina. The church was just five blocks away. There would be plenty of adults at the wedding. Mina knew the church, didn't she? Our Lady of Perpetual Help?

"You can come, too," Lindsay told Mina.

"Do you know the people getting married?" Mina asked.

"No. I just stand outside."

Mina laughed. She said Nicola could go if she took the phone. "I might drop by if I get everything done." She sighed. She was a lawyer, which meant more homework than even Ms. Phibbs could assign.

Nicola and Lindsay headed off, leaving poor June Bug behind.

"But I'm confessing, too, right?" Nicola said, and Lindsay nodded.

For five leaf-strewn blocks Lindsay wondered out loud about the bride's dress. Nicola, who saw no difference between one long white dress and another, didn't say anything. When they reached the old brick church, Lindsay pointed to the marble statue of a lady above the door.

"That's the Lady of Perpetual Help. Perpetual means you can come day or night," she explained.

The wedding guests were arriving, dressed up and laughing. Lindsay fidgeted until a car decorated with paper flowers and streamers pulled up.

"There she is!"

The bride had trouble getting out of the car, she was so tangled up in lace. She needed all four bridesmaids and the flower girl to help her up the steps and into the church. Then Nicola and Lindsay had to wait around for what seemed like another hour while Lindsay praised the dress.

"Did you see the beading on the bodice? My mom's wedding dress had that."

"What's a bodice?" Nicola asked.

"The top of the dress. Bodice, sleeves, skirt and train."

Finally, the wedding march played and everyone came out again, the bride and groom smiling like crazy and kissing everyone gathered on the steps.

"Now," Lindsay said, giving Nicola a poke.

Nicola squeezed through the crowd. She'd only been inside a church once, for her grandma's funeral when she was four. She slipped through the big carved doors and looked around.

Up front stood a table covered with a white cloth. Light shone through one of the stained-glass windows and painted a picture on it. All around the church there were these pretty windows. One showed a golden-haired angel unrolling a scroll.

Peace Be Upon You.

Nicola followed a path of flower petals to a bench in front. She sat and waited, breathing the perfumed air.

After a few minutes, a side door opened and a man appeared, whistling and pushing a broom. He wore jeans and a plaid shirt and, on his belt, a silver knob about the size of a yo-yo with keys dangling from it.

The janitor. He got halfway down the aisle before he noticed Nicola.

"Did they forget the flower girl?"

"No," Nicola said. "I want to talk to the priest."

"Father Mark's gone."

"What?" Nicola cried. "But I came to confess!"

"He just finished a wedding. He's gone for the day."

Nicola folded forward, pressing her forehead against the bench in front.

"Is it that bad?" the janitor asked.

Nicola looked up again. "Yes!"

The janitor leaned the broom against the wall and came and sat in front of her. His eyes were kind and gray.

"Do you want to tell me about it? Get it off your chest. If that doesn't help, you can come back and talk to Father Mark."

"Will it count?" she asked. "I mean, if you're not a priest."

"Why not?" the janitor said.

"Okay. But I should tell you first that I don't even go to church."

He shrugged. "That's not important. Try to be good. That's what I believe."

"What should I call you if you're not the priest?"

"Ignacio. That's my name. What's yours?"

"Nicola. Okay, Ignacio. I have a lot to say." Her eyes got watery at the thought of all the terror and destruction she had to put into words. "I'm not here for myself. I'm confessing for someone else. That's allowed, isn't it?"

"Technically, no," he said. "But I'm not the priest, so go ahead."

"I'm here for June Bug. Can you confess for an animal?"

He drew back. "You're here to confess for a bug?"

"No, my dog. Her name is June Bug. Because she was born in June. Ignacio, she's so bad. She does so many terrible things. She doesn't mean to. I see it in her eyes. She's as shocked as we are when she sees what she's done."

And it gushed out of Nicola. All the shoes June Bug had chewed. The television remote controls she'd carried away and hidden. Julie Walters-Chen.

Ignacio interrupted. "Keep her outside."

"She digs holes. She wrecked the lawn. Dad says it looks like an exploded minefield. Also, she ran away. Twice. Do you see how bad she is? Are these sins, Ignacio?"

"Sins? I don't think you could call them sins, no."

"She steals."

He frowned.

"She steals Jackson's Matchbox cars and eats the wheels. Then she hides them, too. And she smokes."

"Your dog *smokes*?"

Nicola could tell by his shocked expression that smoking was a sin for sure.

"Well, she eats anything on the ground, even cigarette butts. When we catch her, we shout, 'No smoking! No smoking!' Is there such a place as hell, Ignacio?"

He squirmed, like he was sitting on something sharp.

"I'm supposed to say there is. But really? I'm not sure. I think everyone makes his own way in the world as best he can. The real sinners? Thieves and murderers, people like that? I hope they find a way to make amends."

"For dogs, I mean," Nicola said. "Is there a hell for dogs?"

"For dogs? No. I say that with confidence."

"Because I'm worried about June Bug. Jared says that's where she's going."

"She's an animal. She's innocent of sin," Ignacio said. "Whatever June Bug's done, Nicola? Consider it undone. Okay?"

"Really?"

"Really. Feel better?"

She nodded, uncertain.

"Good! Now run home and see what that naughty dog of yours is up to."

"I'm almost afraid to." Nicola stood up. "Thank you."

She walked out, following the trail of flower petals down the aisle. When she glanced back, Ignacio had taken up the broom again and was chuckling to himself.

Outside, the wedding crowd had left. Lindsay was waiting by herself. "How did it go?"

"The priest wasn't there," Nicola said. "Just the janitor."

"That's Ignacio, the manager of our apartment building. He tells me when the weddings are. The priest would be too busy to hear about a dog anyway. So Ignacio's better."

Nicola said, "I just hope he's right. About June Bug not going to hell, I mean."

5

————

PAINTED IN the entranceway of Queen Elizabeth Elementary School, just above the still-crooked picture of the queen, was the school motto.

IS IT FAIR? IS IT SAFE? IS IT KIND?

In October, the kindergarten teacher put up a frieze of construction paper leaves her students had made by outlining their little hands. Only when the frieze went up did people notice that the real leaves on the trees hadn't changed color. One day it got very cold and the next the leaves were black and shriveled. Fall looked ugly, when normally Nicola thought it was the prettiest season.

The school janitor had already got out the ladder for the kindergarten teacher to put up the leaf frieze. Mrs. Dicky didn't want to ask him to get it out again, except the kindergarten teacher had accidentally covered the school motto. You couldn't see anymore when you entered the school that it was a safe, fair and kind place. Also, Mrs. Dicky wanted to straighten the picture of the queen. Several times a week she asked the janitor to do it, but the queen always ended up crooked again.

So that day, Mrs. Dicky decided just to drag a chair out of the office and stand on it.

Which was when she fell.

Nobody saw it happen. But at recess, while everyone was shivering in the early cold staring at the playground equipment they weren't allowed to play on, they saw the ambulance take Mrs. Dicky away.

For several weeks the students and staff of Queen Elizabeth Elementary didn't have a principal. By the time the temporary one came, he had so much catching up to do that there was no winter holiday concert. Some of the classes didn't even have a party.

Ms. Phibbs' class didn't. Instead, they got extra homework for the winter break.

※

Over the holidays June Bug ate or destroyed most of the ornaments on the lower branches of the Christmas tree. She ate the Styrofoam balls that Jackson had pasted with pictures from Christmas cards. June Bug tore apart the Three Wise Men dolls that were Nicola's favorite ornaments, chewing the bead eyes off their wise faces and ripping their stuffing out. Blobs of white stuffing covered the living-room floor the next morning. It looked like it had snowed inside.

Whenever Nicola took June Bug for a walk, Terence, asked — sort of joking, sort of not — for a report on what Christmas decoration had come out the other end of June Bug.

June Bug didn't eat the glass balls because she was a smart dog. Instead she unhooked them with her teeth, dropped them on the floor and batted them around the house like a cat. Nicola checked all the rooms several times a day because her father had said, "Christmas or no Christmas, if anyone ends up in the emergency room with broken glass in their foot, June Bug is spending the holidays at the SPCA."

So Nicola removed all the remaining decorations from the lower branches of the Christmas tree and hung them up higher. The tree looked funny after that, like it had forgotten to put on its pants. Also, there weren't any presents under it. They couldn't trust June Bug not to rip them open. All the presents were closed up in Mina and Terence's bedroom.

After Nicola moved the decorations, several disaster-free days passed. She started to relax and enjoy the holidays. She helped bake the gingerbread. (June Bug *loved* gingerbread. She would Sit and Shake a Paw and Roll Over for gingerbread.) Nicola even went shopping with her mother and, while they were out, forgot completely that she had a bad little dog. Her stomach only started churning when she got home and Mina said, "I wonder what trouble June Bug got into while we were gone."

None! Once the decorations were out of reach, she was almost a good little dog as well as a cute little dog — all white except for her black eye patch, and one black ear and the black leather of her nose.

Nicola had asked for only one Christmas gift — Three More Chances for June Bug.

"You're sure about that?" Terence and Mina asked.

"Yes," Nicola said. The money the family saved by not buying Nicola presents, she wanted put in a special June Bug damage fund, so Jackson could replace any cars June Bug stole, or Terence could buy some grass seed to patch June Bug's holes.

"Ha!" Jared said. "Money isn't going to buy me love."

He was still mad about Julie Walters-Chen. All the hours he wasn't playing on the computer in the den, he spent shut up in his room listening to rap music and tattooing JWC all over his arms with a ballpoint pen.

On Christmas Eve, after everyone had gone to bed, Mina moved the presents. She stacked them under the tree, making a perfect set of stairs to the higher branches.

Then she shut June Bug up in the kitchen so she couldn't get into trouble.

And she wouldn't have, if Terence hadn't got up in the night and wandered sleepily into the kitchen for some gingerbread.

Terence forgot to close the kitchen door.

In the middle of the night, Nicola heard a crash. It sounded like Santa had missed the mark completely and flown into the chimney and knocked it down.

She sprang out of bed. Everyone did. Moments later, the whole Bream family was in the living room, gaping at the tree that lay across the floor like the day it had been chopped down on the tree farm. Little June Bug was leaping over it, joyfully flinging ornaments that, until a minute ago, had been so tormentingly out of reach.

"Now Santa won't come!" Jackson wailed. "Santa won't bring me a present!"

"Look at all the presents," Mina said. "Santa already came."

All the presents were under the fallen tree, lying in a pool of water from the tree stand.

Jared stabbed his finger at Nicola. "Two More Chances! Just Two More Chances for that dog!"

"Stop it!" Terence said. "For heaven's sake! Let's all go back to bed! It's three o'clock in the morning!"

Everyone did, except Nicola, who rescued all the wet presents and set them out of June Bug's reach. She wiped up the puddle of water. Then she sank down by the fallen tree and sobbed while June Bug danced around her, pushing a toy soldier ornament against Nicola's leg, trying to get Nicola to chase her. When Nicola wouldn't, June Bug jumped into Nicola's lap and licked the snot and salty tears off her face.

The next morning, Nicola was up first, even before June Bug, who was still tired from her active night. Half an hour later Terence came into the living room, yawning and tying up his robe. He looked around and saw Nicola curled on the couch waiting for the rest of the family to wake up.

"I was hoping it was a nightmare," he said.

Together, they stood the tree up again.

"Look," Nicola said.

Not a single ornament remained on the branches. The lights, too, were mostly pulled off, lying in loops at the base of the tree. But at the very top the china angel still perched, unbroken, soundlessly blowing its golden horn.

June Bug hadn't touched it.

6

————

NICOLA LAY on her bed with June Bug. From the basement came the repeated smash of Jared practicing kick-flips on his new skateboard in the desperate hope of impressing Julie Walters-Chen. He'd asked for a cellphone and a laptop. The skateboard had been a distant third choice.

In the hall, Jackson's new remote-control car whirred up and down. Every time it neared Nicola's closed bedroom door, June Bug would stop chewing Nicola's braid, stand at attention and bark.

Nicola began humming along to "Hark the Herald Angels Sing" playing on the radio in the kitchen. June Bug stopped chewing again. She tilted her head.

"What is it, June Bug?" Nicola asked.

June Bug tilted her head the other way and her ears twitched. Her tail, stubby and white, thumped the bedspread. June Bug thumped slowly, then faster and faster until she had wound herself up. Then she pounced on Nicola's chest and washed kisses inside her ears and nose until Nicola shrieked with laughter.

"Dinner!" Terence called. "Come and get it!"

Dinner was one of the words June Bug understood, along with her name and the commands Come, Sit, Lie Down, Roll Over, Bang Bang You're Dead, Shake, Wave and Crawl. Despite being such an intelligent animal, June Bug could not seem to make sense of No, Stop, Leave It, Get Down or I'm Going to Kill That Dog Right Now.

June Bug dashed ahead to the dining room and jumped up on Jared's chair.

"Get Down!" Terence commanded.

June Bug didn't. Her face, divided down the middle, white and black, peeped hopefully over the edge of the table at the enormous turkey spilling out stuffing, the Brussels sprouts and mashed potatoes, the steaming gravy in the china boat.

"No, June Bug!" Mina scolded, coming in with the Christmas crackers.

June Bug lifted her nose in the air and sniffed.

"I'm Going to Kill That Dog Right Now!" Jared said, shoving June Bug off his chair and throwing himself on it.

"Don't be so mean!" Nicola cried.

"Put her outside," Mina said.

Nicola didn't want to. It was terribly cold. Despite how much white hair June Bug shed all over the furniture, she hardly seemed to have any on her body. The pink skin of her belly showed right through her skimpy coat.

"Out!" Terence said, and Nicola picked up the squirming dog and carried her to the kitchen door. She shook the snow off the doormat so June Bug would have a more comfortable place to sit while she waited to be let back in.

The Breams popped the Christmas crackers and laughed over the prizes and jokes inside. They put on the colored paper crowns. Then they ate. And ate. Gravy drowned everything, except the trifle. They gobbled up the trifle, then pushed back their chairs, groaning.

"All day to cook," Mina said. "Fifteen minutes to eat."

Nicola, who had saved a bit of everything in the napkin in her lap, hurried to the kitchen door to give June Bug her Christmas dinner.

Snowy pawprints disappeared down the back steps.

"June Bug!" Nicola called. "June Bug, come!"

June Bug did not.

Nicola wanted to look for June Bug right away, but her mother said that June Bug always came back.

This was true. They had to phone Grammy and Grampy in Nova Scotia to wish them a Merry Christmas, and Nicola had to help clean up. Then the Breams were going to play rummy.

"If she's not back after rummy, we'll look," Mina said.

Nicola left the kitchen door open a crack, which she wasn't supposed to do. She wasn't supposed to let the heat out, but she was too worried about June Bug. No one noticed because they were all in the dining room dealing out the cards.

They were well into the game when June Bug came in again, smiling. She was a dog who could smile. She smiled when she dug a hole in the lawn and when she Rolled Over or fell down on her side, Pretending to be Dead. When she did anything she was proud of, she smiled.

Like now, when she backed into the dining room dragging half a snow-covered Christmas turkey.

June Bug parked the turkey at Nicola's feet. It was nearly as big as she was. Jackson saw it first and screamed, "Our turkey! June Bug got our turkey!"

No one else said anything, because what was left of the Breams' turkey was on the kitchen counter.

"June Bug?" Nicola asked in a quavery voice. "Where did you get that turkey?"

"She stole it, obviously," Jared answered. "She stole Christmas dinner right from under someone's nose."

Terence said, "Don't jump to conclusions, young man. Anyway, that looks to me like *half* a turkey. If she did steal it, she only stole the leftovers."

"The leftovers are the best part," Jared said. "Turkey sandwiches the next day? *Someone's* not getting any."

Then June Bug, who had been sitting so proudly listening to what she thought was praise coming from the Breams, flattened her ears in discomfort, took two steps away from the table, and threw up.

"There's the other half!" Jared crowed. He stabbed his finger at Nicola. "Two Chances used up today! One More Chance and that dog is *out of here!*"

✳

Nicola and her mother set off into the frozen night with the remains of their own turkey wrapped in foil and tucked inside Mina's winter coat. They followed June Bug's tracks as best as they could. June Bug was with them, too, being dragged along by her leash. They had hoped that she would lead them to the scene of the crime, but June Bug was not cooperating.

"This is really awful, Nicola," her mother said. "Imagine having your turkey stolen at Christmas. That family's dinner is ruined."

"Is June Bug going to the SPCA?" Nicola asked.

"She's got One More Chance."

"She's still a puppy," Nicola reminded her mother.

"I know she is, sweetheart. It's just that she's pretty much the worst-behaved puppy there ever was."

"She's so cute, though, and so smart." Nicola glanced back at June Bug, who was plowing up the snow behind them with her stiff legs, refusing to walk.

The tracks got mixed up in front of the Durmazes' house. Nicola handed June Bug's leash to Mina, then crept up the front steps. The living-room drapes were partly open. Nicola could see through to the dining room, where everyone was still at the table eating mince pie. She recognized Aleisha, who was in her class. The Durmazes looked too happy to be people whose turkey had been stolen.

Nicola trudged back down the steps. June Bug was sitting on Mina's boots now, shivering.

"Can I take June Bug home?" Nicola asked, but her mother said no.

They looked in the window of every house on the street. If the drapes were closed, there was usually a slit Nicola could peek through. Even if they knew the people, Nicola and Mina were too embarrassed to ring the doorbell and ask if their turkey had gone missing.

"Strange," Mina commented. "Hardly anyone put up Christmas lights this year."

"We didn't," Nicola said.

"You're right. Why didn't we?"

"I guess for the same reason the leaves didn't change color," Nicola said.

"Didn't they?"

"No."

When they got to the end of the block, they watched to see if June Bug would turn left or right or keep going straight. June Bug about-faced and tried to take off for home. Nicola picked her up.

They'd checked half the houses in the neighborhood when a police car pulled along beside them.

"I don't believe it," Mina said.

Nicola was so frightened that she let June Bug go. The dog landed on all fours, lifting one paw at a time off the snowy sidewalk and shaking it.

A police officer stepped out of the car and addressed Mina. "May I ask what you're doing, ma'am?"

"We're trying to return something. Sort of. It can't actually be returned. No one would want it back. But we want to make amends. It's Christmas."

The officer said, "We've received complaints. Suspicious behavior in the neighborhood. Possibly an attempted break-and-enter."

Mina put a gloved hand over her face. "The trouble that dog gets us into!"

"I notice there's something under your coat," he said. "Or are you having twins?"

"It's the rest of our turkey!"

Mina pulled the package out and opened it for the officer. He peered at it to make sure it really was turkey, not someone's silverware.

"Have some," Mina said.

"Mmm," he said, pulling off a piece of meat and tasting it.

Mina tapped on the window of the police car to offer some turkey to the officer behind the wheel. He was wearing a Santa hat. He nodded, and when Mina opened the car door, June Bug leapt right inside and bounced off the passenger seat into the back where the criminals ride.

"Ho-ho!" said the Santa officer. "Someone's in a big hurry to get arrested!"

"She's the guilty one, all right," Mina told him.

"Let's take her down to the station and book her. Get in."

Mina got in the back seat, taking Nicola's hand and pulling her in. Up front, the two officers turned on the siren and the flashing lights. They drove off with June Bug crouched in the back window, bobbing her head exactly like a dashboard ornament.

All the way home Nicola held back her tears, hoping that this wasn't Chance Number Three.

7

_____

LATER THAT night it started snowing. It was still snowing the next morning, Boxing Day, when Nicola walked June Bug over to Our Lady of Perpetual Help Church. Out front, the nativity scene was blanketed in white. All that showed were the heads and shoulders of the three plywood wise men and the plywood angel hovering above them, painted gold.

Nicola didn't really expect to find Ignacio at the church. She only hoped. She hoped, and there he was, shoveling the steps in a big hat with earflaps.

Eventually he noticed June Bug — her black patch, one black ear and two pleading black eyes, emerging from the white blur.

"Your dog is cold," he told Nicola, who was attached to the other end of the leash. "Do you want to bring her inside and warm her up?"

"I don't think we should, Ignacio. I really don't."

Only when she said his name did he recognize her. "You're Lindsay's friend. Nicola, right?"

"She sits beside me at school."

"And this is the bad dog you told me about? You don't think she'd make trouble in a church, do you?"

"I know she will," Nicola said.

Ignacio left the shovel and came down the steps. He asked if he could hold June Bug.

"Be careful," Nicola said. "If she really likes you, she'll bite your nose."

He unzipped his parka and slid the dog's small, shivering body in against his chest. June Bug licked his face.

Nicola got straight to the point. "What you told me before, Ignacio? That dogs don't go to hell? Are you really sure about that?"

"Pretty sure," he said.

"She almost got arrested."

"What? This little creature?" He looked down at June Bug's head poking out so sweetly from under his chin. "I don't believe it."

Nicola nodded. "Yesterday. *Christmas* Day. Anyway, I got another idea. Once there was a scary movie on TV that I wasn't allowed to watch. I wasn't allowed to know anything about it. So of course my brother Jared told me everything and I couldn't sleep for a whole year. It was about a girl who got infected by a devil. She had to be exercised."

"I think you mean exorcised," Ignacio said.

"A priest exercised her," Nicola said.

"How?"

"Jared didn't say. He just said her head turned completely around and the devil left. Do you think June Bug got infected?"

The janitor laughed.

"Could you ask the priest to exercise June Bug? Just in case?"

"Father Mark? I don't think he does that. But I could throw a ball for her," Ignacio said.

"That's not going to do it." Nicola sank to her knees with her mittens pressed together. Huge white flakes floated silently down around her. "Please, Ignacio. She only has One More Chance. Then they'll send her away. She'll go to hell for sure."

Ignacio's face under the earflap hat was already red from shoveling and from the cold. Nicola thought it looked redder now. He asked her to get off her knees. When she refused, he sat on the bottom step and looked at her with his kind gray eyes.

"What do *you* do when you've done a bad thing, Nicola?"

"Yesterday? After June Bug stole someone's turkey? Me and my mom tried to find the people."

"She stole someone's turkey?" He looked shocked.

"Yes! We brought what was left of *our* turkey so they could have Christmas dinner. Also fifty dollars from June Bug's damage fund. Mom said it looked like a fifty-dollar turkey. Well, the part we saw looked like thirty dollars. The other part you couldn't pay someone to take."

"So you tried to do a good deed to make up for it?"

Nicola brightened. "That's a good idea! I'll do something good!"

"Now, Nicola. You already confessed for June Bug, which is fine. She can't talk. But if you do her good deed, too, nothing's going to change. She has to do the good deed herself."

"That's going to be difficult."

"It will be easy! A few minutes ago I turned around and saw June Bug for the first time. You know what I felt? I felt filled with happiness. Just looking at this cute dog made me happy. Looking at her now, warm in my coat? I'm overjoyed! I'm ecstatic!" He threw one arm in the air. The other was holding the dog.

Nicola smiled. "She's good when she's asleep."

"What else is she good at?"

"Besides being bad? Kissing. And she can do tricks."

"Tricks?" Ignacio said. "People take their pets around to hospitals and nursing homes and places like that. You could do that. She could show off her tricks."

"I'd be afraid to take her to a hospital."

"You could try. Do you want to? I'll ask Father Mark if he knows a place. Come back next week, okay?"

Nicola tried not to sound discouraged, but a week was a long time. Long enough for a little dog to do a lot more damage.

Ignacio unzipped his coat and lifted June Bug out. Nicola decided to carry her. Taking her from the warm place next to Ignacio's heart and setting her down in the cold snow seemed cruel.

"See you soon," Ignacio said before he went back up the church steps to finish shoveling. "We'll save June Bug."

"I hope so."

Nicola trudged off with her little dog under her arm, heading in the general direction of home, preoccupied with worry and paying no attention to which street she took. Except for the squeak of her boots in the cold, the whole white world was silent.

June Bug squirmed to be put down.

"There you go," Nicola said.

June Bug started pulling. She pulled and sniffed and made those strange *ork ork ork* sounds that used to frighten Nicola until the vet explained that June Bug wasn't having an asthma attack, but reverse sneezing.

The snow was getting up her nose, but still she sniffed and sneezed and pulled Nicola on, excited about whatever scent she'd picked up.

Until, abruptly, she stopped.

In the snow bank, some child had swished out an angel — a crisp, perfectly outlined impression with a skirt and wings. June Bug sniffed at it and her stubby tail wagged.

Beyond the snow angel was a low concrete building with high windows and a wooden fence. It could have been an office or a small factory, except for the sign:

SHADY OAKS RETIREMENT HOME.

Nicola gave herself a little shake. June Bug did, too, jangling the tags on her collar. She looked at Nicola and tilted her head.

Sometimes it seemed to Nicola that she and June Bug communicated perfectly. Like now. June Bug seemed to have pulled her to the very place they needed.

Now she seemed to be saying, "Let's go in."

"Okay," Nicola said.

No one at the Shady Oaks Retirement Home had recently shoveled. Nicola carried June Bug again, stepping in the old footprints half filled with fresh snow. These led up a wheelchair ramp to the front door, which was glass. In the vestibule, a few coats hung on hooks. An inner glass door faced a desk.

Nicola tried the outer door, but it was locked. She pressed the intercom button — twice, then three times — before an impatient voice answered, "Can I help you?"

"I'm here to talk to someone about visiting. With my dog."

Through the glass doors, Nicola could see a plump woman with dyed blonde hair. Not young, but not old, either. A nurse, Nicola guessed from her pajama-like uniform. She was standing behind the desk, which must have been a nursing station, holding the phone and looking through the glass doors right at June Bug.

The second the nurse laid eyes on the little dog, she smiled, just like Ignacio had said.

The front door buzzed and unlocked with a click.

Nicola put June Bug down in the vestibule and stamped the snow off her boots. June Bug sniffed the doormat madly. To her, a doormat was a list of all the people who had ever been to a place. June Bug seemed very interested in who came and went from Shady Oaks.

The nurse met them at the inner door, which was also locked. When she opened it, an odor washed over Nicola, a combination of disinfectant and pee tinged with something sweet.

"And who have we here?" the nurse cooed to June Bug, who wagged, then almost burst through the nurse's legs and into the building that smelled so awful to Nicola, but obviously not to June Bug.

"What's your dog's name?"

"June Bug."

"Help! Get them out of here!" a man's voice called.

The nurse bent down to pat June Bug. Behind her, Nicola could see an old woman hunched in a wheelchair beside the nursing station. She was wearing a bib, her head tipped forward. Somewhere nearby, commercials blared out of a TV.

"So cute," the nurse said. "He or she?"

"She," Nicola said.

The man called for help again.

"And you want to bring her to visit? I'll have to ask

Mr. Devon. He's the manager. We've been under new management since the summer. There are so many different rules now." She pursed her lips, and Nicola could tell she didn't like these new rules.

Meanwhile, the person calling for help was either coming closer, or yelling louder. "Help!"

"I'll tell you what, sweetheart. What's your name?"

"Nicola."

"Nicola, I'm Jorie. Come back tomorrow. I'll run it by Mr. Devon this afternoon."

Around the corner came an old man in a stretched brown cardigan flecked with dried bits of food. He was bald except for his eyebrows — which were like insect feelers — and the tufts of white hair above and in his ears. The way he walked, stepping with his left leg and dragging the other up to meet it, his right arm dangling, reminded Nicola of a monster in a horror movie.

June Bug rushed over with her usual greeting.

"Who are you?" he boomed at Nicola.

"Mr. Milton," Jorie said in a voice nearly as loud as his. She didn't sound angry. She was trying to soothe him. "This little girl has dropped by with her dog. Maybe you'll get to visit with them tomorrow, if Mr. Devon says it's all right."

Words slurred from the stretched side of his mouth. "Are you a stranger?"

Nicola was too frightened to answer.

Jorie said, "She's not a stranger. Her name is Nicola."

"Do not forget to entertain strangers!" Mr. Milton bellowed.

Jorie patted the old man's shoulder. "We won't, Mr. Milton. We certainly won't."

To Nicola she said, "Sweetie? Come back tomorrow."

Nicola turned to go, pulling June Bug, who seemed to want to stay.

Back outside, Nicola paused on the ramp, gulping air that, though freezing, was at least fresh. Then she and June Bug retraced their steps down the snowy walk, June Bug leaping from footprint to footprint.

They reached the sidewalk and had just turned for home when Nicola heard an ominous thunk behind her. A gray car pulling up at Shady Oaks.

The driver got out, a man dressed in a dark overcoat, a large fur hat like a tea cozy, and tinted glasses. A cigarette dangled from his lips, his exhalations forming clouds in the cold air.

When the man reached the place where the angel was swished out in the snow bank, he stopped, the way Nicola and June Bug had.

What he did next made Nicola cringe.

He stepped on the angel, sinking his boot knee-deep into the snow. He stamped and stamped.

Then he continued up the walk to Shady Oaks Retirement Home.

8

——

BEFORE BED that night Nicola stood in the bathroom brushing her hair. When it was loose, her hair reached her waist. But it was almost never loose because June Bug loved Nicola's braid.

June Bug sat at Nicola's feet now, staring up, so the triangular flaps of her ears fell back. She looked so funny like that, her ears long and Chihuahua-pointed instead of folded like two small silky napkins, one black, one white.

Once Nicola had finished brushing, she braided, weaving the thick sections of hair together over her shoulder.

June Bug shifted from side to side in anticipation.

Nicola secured the end of the braid with the hair elastic.

June Bug bounced.

"Okay, June Bug!"

When Nicola leaned sideways, June Bug sprang and grabbed hold of the braid. Nicola stepped into the hall with the dog hanging on. She got all the way to the kitchen where her mother was working on the giant holiday crossword puzzle, the one that filled two whole newspaper pages.

"I need an eight-letter word for 'heavenly being,'" Mina said, before looking up and frowning. "Nicola, that's fifteen pounds of dog dangling from your braid. It can't be good for your neck."

June Bug let go, thudding four-footedly to the floor.

"Thank you, June Bug," Mina said, returning to the puzzle.

June Bug headed for her pillow in the corner, Nicola for the chair across from her mother. She leaned over and swept the eraser tailings off the newspaper with the end of her braid.

"How did Grandma Bream die?" she asked.

"Cancer. Do you remember much about her?"

"I remember visiting her apartment. I remember her cinnamon buns."

Mina smiled. "She liked to bake."

"And I remember her funeral, sort of. She didn't seem very old."

"She wasn't, unfortunately. Not even seventy."

"Grammy and Grampy don't seem old, either. Not like people in a retirement home."

"Grammy and Grampy are amazing. Seraphim."

"What?"

"That's the eight-letter word for a heavenly being."

Mina searched the vast network of squares for the place to write the word.

"I'd like to take June Bug to visit a retirement home. Is that okay?"

Nicola half-wished that her mother would say no. Shady Oaks smelled bad, and the old man, Mr. Milton, frightened her with his booming voice and the strange things he said. Even worse was that man stomping on the snow angel.

Except if Mina did say no, June Bug would have to wait until the priest found her a different place to do a good deed.

"What retirement home?" Mina asked.

"It's called Shady Oaks. It's over by the church."

"What church?"

"Our Lady of Perpetual Help. You remember. I went there with that girl Lindsay."

"Does the retirement home have anything to do with the church?"

"No," Nicola said, in case her mother was heading toward an Embarrassing Talk.

Nicola had suffered through several of these. The Embarrassing Talk about Where Babies Come From. The Embarrassing Talk about What Your Big Brother Is Going Through and Why He Is So Mean. Nicola would rather not have known the facts in these Embarrassing Talks. She wasn't planning on making babies, not after living with Jackson. And after living with

Jared, she was never going to have anything to do with boys.

"I stopped there today when I was walking June Bug and asked if I could bring her. They said to come back tomorrow."

"You already went? On your own?" Mina pushed the puzzle aside. "Nicola. We talked about this."

Nicola hung her head. That was the talk about the Bad People Who Would Just Love to Get Their Hands on Unattended Children, which was not so much Embarrassing as Terrifying. She fiddled with the end of her braid.

"So you've already organized this visit?"

"Yes. I want June Bug to cheer up the old people. I'm hoping it will make up for the turkey and the tree and everything else. I'm hoping it will make her a good, kind dog who won't get in so much trouble."

"That's lovely, Nicola," Mina said. "I'm proud of you. Certainly you can go."

Nicola smiled the way you do when you get something you don't want very much. A small smile.

"But I'd like to go with you the first time."

"That would be great," Nicola said, brightening.

"And I'd like you to bring a friend."

Nicola slumped. "Who?"

"Are you still not talking to Mackenzie?"

"She has other friends now."

"What about Lindsay?"

"She's not really a friend," Nicola said. "She just sits next to me in school. She loves flowers and brides. And she follows me around at school, which is annoying."

"It sounds like she wants to be friends with *you*." Mina pointed across the kitchen. "The class list is in that drawer."

Nicola found the list with the phone numbers. She took it to the den where Jared was playing on the computer. He kept the phone with him at all times, even in the bathroom. Even with Nicola telling him through the door, "I don't think Julie Walters-Chen would be too impressed if she found out you were sitting on the toilet while you talked to her!"

"Don't tie up the line," Jared said now.

Nicola stuck out her tongue and went to the living room to call.

Lindsay answered, sounding so happy that Nicola had phoned. "What did you get for Christmas?"

"Nothing," Nicola said. "I didn't want anything."

"Really?"

"Really."

"The best thing I got," Lindsay said, "was a subscription to *Today's Bride*."

Nicola sighed. "Can you give Ignacio a message? He was going to help me find a place to visit with June Bug. But I found a place myself."

"What place?"

"A retirement home. I'm going to take June Bug to do her tricks."

"Oh," Lindsay cried. "*That* sounds like fun! Can I come? Please?"

9

———

JORIE BUZZED them in — Mina and the girls and June Bug. She smiled until she saw Lindsay's bouquet, crazy in a good way, crammed with every type of flower. "Oh, dear."

"My mom's a florist," Lindsay said. "She lets me have the leftovers. I arranged it myself."

"Give it to me," said a younger nurse who was filling little paper cups with pills from bottles lined up on the counter. She was taller than Jorie, her light brown hair in a high ponytail. She took the bouquet from Lindsay and practically flung it on the nursing station counter without even putting it in water.

All the while, June Bug tugged on the leash wrapped twice around Nicola's hand, trying to make a break for the hall. The disinfectant-pee smell was just as strong today.

While Mina and Jorie chatted, Nicola read the names on the pill bottles. She smiled at the nurse filling the cups. The nurse frowned back. Lindsay just stood there, trying not to breathe, or so it seemed.

"I told the manager she was coming," Jorie told Mina. "You should know he wasn't thrilled. He'll be less thrilled about two girls."

"Maybe they shouldn't stay," Mina said.

"No, no. It will be such a treat for the dears. I'm just saying in case he shows his face. He manages several homes in the city so they might not even see him."

The nurse who was filling the pill cups piped up, "She said she would quit if they couldn't come."

"I'd quit anyway if it wasn't for the dears," Jorie said. "I've been working here three years. Then this past summer the place was sold to a chain. Mr. Devon's running all their homes. So, Nicola? Don't mind Mr. Devon if he shows up scowling and frowning. You won't be doing anything wrong. That's just how his face looks."

The other nurse laughed bitterly.

"Do you want to stay?" Mina asked them, glancing around the place and sniffing.

Beside the nursing station was a lounge where a TV played the Shopping Channel. Three old people were there — one asleep in her wheelchair in front of the TV, one sitting at a table staring at a balled-up tissue, and a third very thin woman in an armchair talking to herself.

Lindsay, her hand over her mouth and nose, stared through the pink frames of her glasses at the old people who didn't seem to notice each other, let alone visitors with a dog.

"June Bug wants to cheer everyone up," Nicola said, meaning she would stay, no matter how bad it smelled.

"I'll see you in about an hour then," Mina said.

"You're leaving?" Nicola asked.

"I've got so much work."

Jorie buzzed Mina out. Lindsay watched forlornly, but followed Jorie when she led them to the lounge.

It was only two days after Christmas, but there wasn't a tree. No decorations of any kind. Not even pictures on the wall, or plants. Just the blaring TV advertising a special cloth called the ShamTastic that could absorb twice the amount of spilled liquid as a regular cloth.

They went over to the old man sitting at the table. June Bug, who was much more interested in continuing down the hall, had to be dragged.

"Look, Mr. Eagleton!" Jorie said to him. "We have visitors today! These two girls. Nicola and — what's your name, sweetie?"

"Lindsay."

Mr. Eagleton, who had gray hair and an unwashed smell, continued to gaze at the tissue on the table like it was a crystal ball. He didn't react until Jorie touched his shoulder. Then he looked up in slow motion and blinked at her with watery eyes.

"Can you pick her up?" Jorie asked Nicola, who scooped up June Bug and held her in front of the old man's face. His expression didn't change when June

Bug stretched her neck out to lick him, but his mouth fell open.

"Do you want to say something, Mr. Eagleton?" Jorie asked.

He did, but he took a very long time to do it.

Finally, all three sounds dribbled out. "P...U...P." They could hardly hear them for the excitement of the woman on the TV demonstrating the ShamTastic.

"Mr. Eagleton," Jorie said, "I am most impressed! Did you hear that, Glenda?" she asked the other nurse, who was approaching with a tray of medications.

Glenda grunted.

Jorie told the girls, "Mr. Eagleton hasn't spoken for three months."

"Doesn't anyone visit him?" Lindsay asked, as they moved to the old woman slumped in front of the Sham-Tastic commercial. She was the same bibbed woman Nicola had seen the day before.

"It's hard for families when their loved ones don't know them anymore. So, no. They don't visit very often."

"Or ever," Glenda chirped.

Lindsay said, "That's terrible."

There were other smells, too. Nicola placed them now. The smell of nothing ever happening. The smell of being lonely and forgotten and confused.

The bib woman wouldn't wake up so they took June Bug over to the woman in the armchair, whose gray hair stuck out all over her head. Jorie called her Mrs. Cream.

"Decimand," she muttered, smiling and looking pleased. "Decimand. Decimand."

"What does 'decimand' mean?" Lindsay asked.

"It doesn't mean anything," Jorie said.

"Then why is she saying it?" Lindsay's face had turned the same color as her glasses frames.

"It's her condition, sweetie."

"Decimand!" Mrs. Cream exclaimed when June Bug was lifted up for her to see. With a thin shaking hand, she patted the top of June Bug's head.

"Are you strangers?" a voice bellowed behind them. They all swung around, June Bug still in Nicola's arms.

"There he goes again," sighed Glenda, who was helping Mr. Eagleton swallow his pills.

The old man from yesterday, Mr. Milton, staggered straight for Nicola, staring. His eyes were bright blue under the spiky feeler brows.

Nicola set June Bug on the floor, expecting the dog to rush over and greet the old man making his monsterish way toward them — one step, then a pause while he dragged the other leg forward.

Instead, June Bug shot past Mr. Milton and down the hall, dragging her leash behind her.

"Mr. Milton," Jorie said, linking her arm with his unmoving one. "She's not a stranger. It's Nicola, who you met yesterday. Remember? And her friend Lindsay."

Lindsay shrank back.

"Nicola's little dog is going to … Goodness. Where did the dog get to?"

Nicola pointed in the direction June Bug had disappeared, then hurried off with Lindsay trailing.

Beyond the nursing station was a long, slippery hallway lined with doors, all of them closed. Before one of them, June Bug was sniffing, making deep snorkeling sounds, trying to figure out the odors. Even Nicola, who couldn't smell half as well, noticed the flowery perfume.

"What's she doing?" Lindsay asked.

"There's something in there she wants," Nicola said. "It must be the kitchen."

Before Nicola could grab June Bug's leash, the dog tore off again. She slowed briefly to sniff under the next door, then ran on.

At the third door, she scratched the way she did when her ball or one of Jackson's Matchbox cars rolled under the furniture.

Nicola caught the leash just as Jorie came around the corner. Immediately, June Bug started pulling Nicola back over to the first door.

"Is this the kitchen?" Nicola asked Jorie.

"It's Mr. Fitzpatrick's room."

"Can she meet him?" Nicola asked.

"Mr. Devon said not to disturb anyone sleeping. I'm pretty sure Mr. Fitzpatrick's sleeping. It's all he does."

The slow-moving Mr. Milton reached them then. He lifted his good arm in its baggy flecked cardigan and pointed at the door.

"Help! Get them out!"

"This was what I was afraid of, girls," Jorie said. "He gets so agitated."

"Help!" he boomed, as Glenda came brisking around the corner with a little paper cup of pills in one hand and a glass of water in another.

"Pill time, Mr. Milton," she sang out to him.

Mr. Milton looked right at Nicola. "Help! Don't forget!"

"You girls wait at the front," Jorie said. "I'll buzz you out as soon as we get him settled."

Nicola and Lindsay watched the green pajama-ed pair lead Mr. Milton down the hall. They turned to go.

On their way to the front entrance, pulling the reluctant dog, they passed the nursing station. Behind the counter were the stools where Jorie and Glenda sat, cupboards and file cabinets. A phone. A wastebasket.

And filling the whole wastebasket was the bouquet Lindsay had brought, stuffed in head first.

Lindsay shrieked when she saw it. "That's the meanest thing I've ever seen! And this is the awfullest place!"

In the lounge, Mrs. Cream and Mr. Eagleton slowly swiveled their heads and stared.

Then Glenda appeared. Lindsay pointed to the discarded bouquet.

Glenda shrugged. "Flowers aren't allowed."

"But why not?"

"Because Mr. Devon said. He makes the rules. I just follow them."

"Is he allergic?" Lindsay asked.

"He's either allergic, or he really, really hates flowers."

Glenda stepped behind the nursing station counter and pressed the buzzer to unlock the doors.

The two girls dressed in the vestibule. "That didn't go so well," Nicola said.

She invited Lindsay to come over and plan what to do the next day.

Lindsay said no. "I'm going home to lie in my Feel Better Box."

10

———

WHEN NICOLA called Lindsay later that day, Lindsay said she wouldn't go back.

"We have to," Nicola explained. "That wasn't enough of a good deed. June Bug didn't even do her tricks."

"That one old man spoke. He hadn't spoken for three months, Jorie said."

"June Bug stole someone's turkey on Christmas Day. Do you realize that?"

Nicola thought she heard Lindsay gasp.

As Nicola was telling Lindsay this, June Bug was curled in a ball on her pillow in the corner of the kitchen, snoring lightly.

"We could put on a show," Nicola said.

Lindsay asked if Nicola had done any of the homework Ms. Phibbs had assigned.

"Some," Nicola said.

"Ten pages of math. I haven't done any. And the wildlife PowerPoint project? Mine's on squirrels. I haven't even started."

"The thing is, I'm not allowed to go alone. My mom said."

Silence.

"Never mind." Nicola hung up.

Just then Jared came into the kitchen and stood with his back to Nicola, propping open the fridge door and letting out the cold while he glugged straight from the milk carton. He'd been told so many times not to do either of these things that Nicola didn't bother repeating it.

Homework.

She snapped to and made a dash for the door, but Jared was too fast. He slammed the fridge and blocked her way so he could get to the computer first.

"Mom!" Nicola screeched.

"I'm putting Jackson to bed," she called from upstairs.

Nicola stomped to the den and stood behind Jared. JWC, JWC, JWC was scribbled in Sharpie up to his elbows. His fingers pounded the keys.

Winged creatures were dropping from the top of the screen. Jared, jaw set, teeth gritted, let loose a barrage of flaming missiles. He tapped and rolled the mouse.

"What do you want?" he eventually grunted.

"I have to work on my PowerPoint!"

One of the winged creatures burst into flame. It plunged from the top of the screen to the bottom while Jared tapped to dodge the satellites and asteroids and space junk floating by.

"You're so annoying."

"I'm going to stay right here until you get off."

"You're going to watch Inferno 2?" he said. "It's *really* violent."

"If it's really violent, you shouldn't play it," Nicola said.

She leaned over his shoulder. Jared left off tapping for a second so he could jab her with his elbow. Something exploded in the middle of the screen, between the upper rings of circles and the lower.

"Now look what you did!"

"What did I do?" Nicola asked.

"I'm trying to guide all my Principalities into the Second Circle! Now I lost one. He gets demoted to an Archangel! Can you get out?"

"What are those circles at the top?"

"The orders of angels."

"And the bottom circles?"

"The circles of hell."

"What's the point?"

"To make every angel fall to the bottom."

Now his left hand came to life and began hammering the keyboard at the same time his right clicked the mouse.

"Why are you doing that?" Nicola asked.

"What?"

"Hitting that key over and over?"

"It's an Extraterrestrial Bombardment! I'm deleting

them. See them? See them swarming in? Die!" Jared yelled, blasting away. "Die!"

Mina poked her head in the door. "What is it, Nicola?"

Just then Nicola got an idea. She swung around.

"Lindsay can't go with me to Shady Oaks tomorrow. Can Jared take me instead?"

✳

Jared wasn't happy. Not at all. But Mina and Terence said there would be consequences if he didn't take his little sister to the retirement home. The consequences were unbearable: no computer *for the rest of the holidays*.

"It's not like I *really* want to go, either," Nicola told him on the march over in the cold. "It's the awfullest sad place I've ever been. But that's the point, right? For June Bug to make it better."

Jared pulled his iPod from his pocket and thumbed the volume louder.

Once Jorie had let them in, Jared threw himself in a plastic chair by the nursing station and pulled his toque low over his eyes. Tinny rap music seeped out through the wool.

Jorie in yellow, and Glenda in pink, were getting the day's meals organized, receiving a shipment of boxes at the back door, loading them onto a trolley. Nicola took

June Bug around to the patients in the lounge and got her to Wave and Shake a Paw, without much response. Mr. Milton was nowhere to be seen.

Afterward, she stopped Jorie in the hall and asked about putting on a proper show for everyone.

"This isn't the best time, sweetie."

"Can we visit Mr. Fitzpatrick then? We've never met him."

"Look in on Mr. Milton," Jorie told her.

Nervously, Nicola went to his room. She tapped on his door.

"Go on in," Jorie called. "He's having a quiet day."

Mr. Milton's room didn't smell of flowers like the hallway, but of something old and abandoned. That something was Mr. Milton in the bed. Loud and menacing the day before, he was dozing now, though his eyes opened briefly when Nicola and June Bug came in.

"Hello, Mr. Milton. It's us. Nicola and June Bug."

Here, too, there were no pictures or knickknacks. The hospital bed and a small wheeled table were the only furniture.

June Bug leapt up on the bed and wagged. Mr. Milton's eyelids fluttered.

Then Glenda came in, her ponytail swinging. She carried a small cardboard box, a glass of water and pills in a tiny paper cup, all of which she set on the wheeled table.

"Lunch time! Wakey, wakey."

She opened the cardboard box. Two circles of bun enclosed a dry puck of meat. Celery wilted on the side. Nicola hated celery. Still, she had to hold June Bug's leash tight because the dog was already straining for the hamburger. Disgusting as it was, it was still People Food.

"Sorry, Mr. Milton," Glenda said. "It's the same as yesterday."

"They have the same lunch every day?" Nicola asked.

"Practically. Now and then a cheese sandwich shows up. And get this. They fly it in from Colorado. Jorie said they used to have a kitchen here, but supposedly this is cheaper. Some of them just won't eat."

Mr. Milton's groggy eyes opened and shifted to the cardboard lunch box. He closed them again as if he'd seen something too awful to contemplate. Glenda helped him swallow the four pills.

"That's the way, Mr. Milton," she told him. "Good job."

"What are the pills for?" Nicola asked.

"Don't ask me. I'm not a doctor." Glenda pushed the table so that the hamburger box was in front of him, then left.

As soon as she was gone, Mr. Milton's blue eyes opened and stared straight into Nicola's. She could tell he was trying very hard to keep them open. His mouth drooped lower.

"Mr. Milton?" Nicola asked, pushing aside the table

so she could sit on the edge of the bed beside June Bug. "Would you like something different to eat?"

She opened June Bug's treat container and shook some treats into her hand.

"I know people don't usually eat dog treats, but really? Organic dog pepperoni is actually better than people pepperoni. It's the same thing, but not so spicy. I love it. Look."

Nicola ate a piece. Mr. Milton watched her chew. So did June Bug, who whimpered for her to share.

"Yum," Nicola said. "But if you don't want to eat it, I understand. You still have your own lunch."

A tear rolled down one of his rough cheeks.

"Don't cry, Mr. Milton. I'm sorry. I won't make you eat dog treats. I probably insulted you. I didn't mean to."

There wasn't even a box of tissues in the room. Nicola had to brush away his tears with the end of her braid. His head moved slightly. It could have been a tremor, except that his mouth opened crookedly.

"You want one?"

She took a piece and slipped it between his dry lips. He chewed in slow motion, swallowed, opened his mouth again.

"See? It's really good!"

Nicola fed him another piece. Then she fed one to June Bug, who was Waving her paw like she was conducting an orchestra. Mr. Milton swallowed and his lips seemed to form a word. She leaned in closer.

"Entertain," it sounded like.

When he'd eaten all the treats in the container, he closed his eyes and fell asleep. Nicola picked up June Bug and tiptoed out of the room.

At the nursing station, Jared sprang up from his chair. "Finally!"

Jorie was in the lounge, helping the patients eat their lunch. She came and buzzed Nicola and Jared out.

Jared bolted ahead, but Nicola stopped to ask, "Could we put on a show tomorrow?"

Jorie said, "I'm not working tomorrow. Pierre is."

"Okay. I'll ask him."

By the time Nicola and June Bug stepped outside, Jared was already at the end of the walk.

"Wait!" she called, but he couldn't hear her with his earbuds in.

She and June Bug caught up and Nicola yanked out one of his wires, which made him even more furious.

"Are you coming back with me tomorrow?"

"Are you nuts? That place stinks. I'm going home to take a shower. Ten showers."

"You need ten showers," she said.

In the next block, he slowed enough to shout over his shoulder. "If I missed a phone call because I had to sit for an hour in that stinking place, I'm going to kill you and that dog!"

Nicola felt sorry for him then. Julie Walters-Chen was never going to call him. Even Jared must have known that. And Nicola remembered what her mother had said during the Embarrassing Talk about What Your Older Brother Is Going Through and Why He Is So Mean. She'd said to try — please, please try — not to be mean back.

"Thank you for coming," Nicola called. "It makes me really sad to go there, too. But I have to."

Jared grunted and walked on, all hunched and pimply, with the toque pulled low. The one earbud swung freely behind his back. Nicola fell in step beside him with June Bug trotting along in front.

"I hope Grammy and Grampy don't end up in a place like that. I hope they'll come and live with us instead."

"They will," Jared said.

"What?" Nicola said.

"End up in a place like that. And so will Mom and Dad. And so will you. We'll all end up like that. We'll all end up in hell."

When Jared said that, even though she knew he didn't mean it, Nicola shuddered. Hormones made him say it. That's what Mina had told her during the Talk.

Nicola didn't plan on ever having Hormones.

✳

While Nicola was making herself a sandwich for lunch, Lindsay dropped by.

"Too late," Nicola told her when she answered the door. "My brother came with me."

Behind her glasses, Lindsay's eyes showed relief, then hope. Hope that Nicola would invite her in, which Nicola pretty much had to since Lindsay wasn't budging from the porch.

They went to the kitchen.

"Are you going to Shady Oaks every single day?" Lindsay asked.

Nicola nodded. "Until the holidays are over."

She brought her sandwich to the table. The second the two girls sat, June Bug dashed over and sprang up on a chair, too. She made a cat noise.

"Do you want lunch, June Bug?"

Nicola stood up. June Bug placed her front paws on the table and leaned closer to the unguarded sandwich. Nicola caught her just in time, scolding June Bug until she laid back her ears and sat properly on the chair again.

Lindsay watched all this, then said, "I have a very sensitive nose." She pointed to her nose, the perch for her pink glasses. "I gag when I smell bad things. Even when I see things that look like they might smell bad. I could never get a dog because there's no way I could pick up the poo."

At the counter, Nicola thickly buttered a piece of

bread. She shook some kibble from June Bug's bowl onto the bread. The butter made the kibbles stick.

"You get used to poop. And when it's your dog, it's not so bad. June Bug's poops are cute. Here, June Bug."

Nicola set the sandwich in front of her dog. June Bug lunged for it.

"It's because my mom's a florist," Lindsay said. "I'm used to nice-smelling things. Also? People suffering? I can't stand it. Or mean things, like what Glenda did to my bouquet. Yesterday, I had to *sleep* in my Feel Better Box."

"What's a Feel Better Box?" Nicola asked.

"Come to my place and I'll show you."

Nicola wasn't visiting a bride-and-flowers girl's house if she wasn't going to help save June Bug.

"I have homework," she said.

"We could do it together."

Lindsay sat there twisting her hands until June Bug burped and leapt off the chair. Lindsay couldn't help but laugh.

"Okay," she said. "I'll try one more time."

11

"WE'RE SET TO break some records this month," the meteorologist announced on the radio the next morning. "Coldest continuous temperature. Greatest snowfall."

"She sounds so cheerful," Mina grumbled at breakfast.

"It's as cold as a dog's nose," Terence said, reaching down to pat June Bug, who was sitting under the table, hoping for crumbs.

"As cold as the devil's heart," Mina said, getting up to pour more coffee.

"A cold day in hell," Jared said.

"Hell?" Jackson piped up, his mouth full of cereal.

"There's that word again," Terence warned.

"You started it," Jared said.

"And no computer until you shovel, young man."

After breakfast, Nicola pulled ski pants over her jeans where the long window beside the door was coated with frost. She and June Bug braced themselves before setting out to meet Lindsay at Shady Oaks. They trotted all the way just to keep from freezing.

Pierre was at the nursing station, a huge man with earrings and hair in cornrows. He came out from behind the desk and fussed over June Bug, scratching behind her ears and up and down her back.

Glenda was working, too.

"Guess what?" she told Lindsay and Nicola. "It's Bath Day. Once a month whether they need it or not."

When Pierre straightened, June Bug leapt against his legs.

"Can she ever jump!"

Nicola said, "She can do tricks, too. Can we put on a show for everyone? I think it would really cheer them up."

Glenda said to Pierre, "I bet he says no."

He, Nicola guessed, was Mr. Devon.

"I have to get them out of bed for their baths anyway," Pierre said. "Mrs. Michaels and Mr. Fitzpatrick are already in their chairs. Is he here?"

Glenda went over to the phone and pressed a button. "Probably not, but you can never tell. He keeps that office door shut." After a minute, she hung up and said, "If he's not here and there's no rule against putting on a dog show —"

"Let's see," Pierre said, counting on his fingers. "No music. No singing."

"No laughing," Glenda said.

"No laughing. Nope, no rule about dog shows."

Glenda stepped into the lounge to fetch the woman

with the bib who was sleeping in front of the blaring TV.

"Come on, Miss Higgins. Let's have some fun for a change." She wheeled the chair down the hall, waving the girls along.

They went to the room Glenda said was for physiotherapy, which was completely bare and brightly lit with fluorescent lights. Glenda parked Miss Higgins and left to get another patient. June Bug sniffed all around where the glaring white walls met the shiny floor. There was nothing else to sniff or even look at. The windows were too high to see out.

Pierre came in holding Mrs. Cream's — the Decimand woman's — arm. He took some folding chairs from the closet, set them up on either side of Miss Higgins' wheelchair and helped Mrs. Cream sit. She looked around brightly, chirping her word.

Meanwhile, June Bug raced over and jumped against Pierre's legs, beating her tail, as though she hadn't seen him for a year. She sproinged and sproinged, each time licking his face, until —

"Ouch!" He straightened, cupping his nose.

"June Bug! No!" Nicola cried. "It means she likes you."

"She won't bite the patients, will she?" Pierre asked. "These folks we're bringing in, they're frail."

Through the propped-open door one came now, in a wheelchair steered by a smiling Glenda.

Nicola had never seen Glenda smile.

"Here's Mrs. Michaels," she said.

Mrs. Michaels was dressed in a thick pink bathrobe many sizes too large, the fabric humped up on her back, pushing her forward in the chair so only the silvery crown of her head showed. Glenda wheeled her into the row and put on the brake.

"Mrs. Michaels?" She patted one of the tiny hands, limp in the lap of the pink robe. "Wakey, wakey."

Gently, she lifted the old woman's chin.

"Oh!" Lindsay cried. "She's beautiful!"

"Isn't she?" Glenda said.

Nicola thought so, too. Mrs. Michaels had the face of a china doll. Her eyes were closed, her lashes white fringes on her smooth cheeks.

June Bug raised her snout, sniffing the sweetening air. She began creeping forward on her leash, ears back, her tail between her legs.

Though June Bug had failed obedience class, Nicola had learned a lot. She'd learned, for example, how dogs ordered themselves according to importance. When two dogs met, the more important dog, the "dominant" one, stayed standing, while the lesser one, the "submissive" dog, sat. It looked almost like a curtsy.

This was exactly what June Bug did now. She crept closer to Mrs. Michaels and when she reached the footplate of the wheelchair where a pair of much-too-large plush slippers roosted, she sat.

Nicola was astonished, because normally, if anyone wore slippers, June Bug would attack them. The Breams wore woolen socks instead of slippers so they could move freely through the house.

June Bug sat on the floor in front of Mrs. Michaels. She kept her gaze lowered. Her black ear and her white ear flattened against her head. Then she fell onto her side and rolled over, showing Mrs. Michaels her bare pink stomach.

Lindsay asked, "Is she sick?"

June Bug seemed to be waiting for Mrs. Michaels' permission to get up. She might have lain there a long time had another patient not been wheeled through the door.

It was a man this time, in a blue robe, with hair as silvery as Mrs. Michaels' and, like her, he was humped and asleep. June Bug sprang to her four feet and started creeping toward the newcomer, ears back, tail tucked in again. She didn't bother sitting. This time, she just flung herself onto her back.

"This is Mr. Fitzpatrick," Pierre said. "He's a fine old gentleman. Doesn't say much. Sleeps a lot. But I feel so good whenever I'm around him. Don't I, sir? Aren't I always telling you that?"

Nicola looked over at Lindsay. Lindsay felt it, too, Nicola could tell. Lindsay was smiling her head off.

Glenda wheeled in another patient, an old woman judging by the pink of the robe. She was tinier than the other two, with a sweet Japanese face.

"Mrs. Tanaka," Glenda said.

Glenda did an amazing thing then. She bent down and kissed the silky top of Mrs. Tanaka's head.

"She is the sweetest person ever. Isn't she, Pierre?"

"I love her," said Pierre.

Again, June Bug crept over and threw herself down.

Now Nicola knew for sure the flowery smell was coming from the patients. It grew stronger with each arrival. Also, the fluorescent lights seemed to be ringing in a way she hadn't noticed before, like a wet finger circling the rim of a wine glass. A faint, singing note.

With the quiet, persistent ringing and the sweet perfume, Nicola felt a little dizzy, like her head was filled with birds. Swooping birds writing in the air. Writing something joyful.

She looked at her little dog, so well behaved, and was filled with love for her, though she loved June Bug just as much when she was bad. Nicola felt such a great gush of love that it was more than any little dog would need, so when she looked at Lindsay and Glenda, and all the patients, she had enough love left over for them. Nicola loved poor Mr. Eagleton and Mr. Milton, too, whom Pierre brought in now, Mr. Eagleton shuffling beside Mr. Milton in a wheelchair.

As soon as June Bug saw Mr. Eagleton and Mr. Milton, she ran to them, wagging her usual greeting. Nicola grabbed the leash just in time.

She stood before the seven old people, half of them bundled and asleep.

"Good morning," she began. "Welcome to June Bug's show. Are you ready to see some amazing tricks?"

Sit. Give Me Five. Shake a Paw.

Nicola even got June Bug to hang from her braid.

✳

The good feeling stayed even after the show was over and the girls and the star of the show left Shady Oaks.

"Something happened," Lindsay said, and Nicola knew instantly what she meant.

Something *had* happened. Something special. Nicola felt it. And it had nothing to do with June Bug's tricks.

They walked in silence for a few minutes, savoring that feeling that had no name.

Then Lindsay asked, "What was the matter with Mr. Milton?"

During the show, Mr. Milton's head hung down. He completely ignored June Bug Rolling Over and Waving and Pretending to be Dead.

Nicola remembered his word the day before. Entertain.

So why hadn't he noticed June Bug trying to entertain him?

12

THE NEXT DAY the Breams went skiing on the trails down by the lake.

"I'm freezing!" Jackson wailed. "I want to go home!"

"You'll warm up once we get moving," Mina said.

They didn't bring June Bug, though Nicola had begged to. She hated the thought of her little dog shut up in the kitchen at home. Dogs were pack animals. They didn't like to be alone.

But it really was bitterly cold.

After a quarter of an hour of skiing, Nicola didn't feel any warmer. Her fingers and toes were numb, her nose a frozen strawberry. By then Jared and Mina were far ahead, Terence and Jackson far behind. Nicola may as well have been skiing alone in some vast silvery landscape. Everything was so quiet, except for her own breathing and the swishing of her skis.

She looked around and marveled how the world in winter seemed made of tiny stars — snowflakes — sunlight glinting off them. A million diamonds couldn't be as beautiful.

And out of the sparkling silvery whiteness of that picture, she remembered a face, even though she'd only seen it for a moment.

Mrs. Michaels.

A warmth seeped through her. Soon all her feeling was restored, even in her nose.

＊

It was partly that face that made Nicola want to go back. Now that she'd seen the silver-haired three shut up in their rooms — Mrs. Michaels, Mr. Fitzpatrick and Mrs. Tanaka — she was curious about them. She knew Lindsay was, too.

Nicola also hoped that Mr. Milton would wake up enough to pay attention to June Bug's tricks. June Bug would be doing such a good deed then. It would make up for all the bad things she had done, if she could entertain him the way he'd asked.

But when they arrived the next day, Nicola's pockets stuffed with gingerbread she'd brought for Mr. Milton, Jorie told them, "Not a good day for Mr. Milton, sweeties. Something's upset him. He's been ranting about strangers all morning. Maybe Glenda messed up his medications. Anyway, he's finally sleeping now."

"Why does he keep talking about the same thing?" Lindsay asked.

"He had a stroke. It affected his brain. That's why he

can't move his right side or properly use his words. He wasn't speaking at all when he came here, so he's actually improved."

"Can we visit Mrs. Michaels? Or Mrs. Tanaka? Or Mr. Fitzgerald?" Lindsay asked. "We met them yesterday."

Jorie looked surprised. "Did you? Did Mr. Devon give his permission?"

Seeing the blush on their faces, Jorie's lips tightened and she shook her head. Then, after a nervous glance around, she whispered to the girls, "Aren't those three lovely?"

Pierre came down the hall carrying a tray with three plastic bowls on it.

"Is that my favorite dog?" he called, and June Bug pulled toward him on her leash.

"Oh, good," Jorie said. "Can you let the girls out when they're ready, Pierre? They're just going to pop into the lounge for a quick visit."

"You don't want to leave, do you, June Bug?" Pierre said, sinking down to the dog's level. He set the tray on the floor so he could use both hands to scratch June Bug all over. One of the bowls was still half full of some unappetizing beige mush.

"Was it hard to train her?" Pierre asked Nicola.

"No. She's so smart."

Pierre gave June Bug one last vigorous scratch and stood. He began a long story about a friend who had taught his dog to Wipe Its Nose by putting a clothespin on its whiskers.

Lindsay nudged Nicola, who looked down just as June Bug licked out the last of the bowls on the tray on the floor.

"No, June Bug!" Nicola cried.

"June Bug!" Pierre said. "You can even wash dishes!"

They made their visit to the lounge. June Bug Waved at Miss Higgins and Mrs. Cream. Nicola lifted her up to Kiss Mr. Eagleton. Then Pierre buzzed them out.

Back in the cold, Nicola offered Lindsay some gingerbread. "I brought it for Mr. Milton. I saw what they gave him for lunch. He liked dog pepperoni better."

June Bug showed no interest in the gingerbread now, which was strange. Even stranger was the way she walked so slowly beside Nicola all the way down the walk, as though Nicola had given her the command to Heel, which she hadn't. Nicola had long given up on Heel. Normally, June Bug either strained at the leash well ahead of Nicola, or had to be dragged behind.

Now she staggered beside Nicola, trying to keep up.

Nicola and Lindsay said goodbye.

"Thanks for coming," Nicola said.

The rest of the way home, June Bug Heeled. Heeled and knocked into the side of Nicola's leg. When they got within sight of the house, instead of pulling Nicola up the walk, June Bug began to stumble. Instead of bounding up the steps three at a time, she sank onto the icy concrete and sighed as though Nicola was expecting her to climb Mount Everest.

"June Bug," Nicola said. "Do you actually need me to carry you up the steps?"

June Bug looked at Nicola with black, dreamy eyes. So Nicola picked her up.

13

_____

NORMALLY WHEN anyone swept the kitchen floor, June Bug would race in from wherever she was making trouble to leap on the broom, her great enemy. Sweeping in the Bream household was all about pushing a little dog around on the end of a long stick.

But today when Terence swept the kitchen, June Bug didn't stir from her corner pillow. So he went ahead and *washed* the floor, too, which had never even been attempted with June Bug in the house.

Then Jackson set up his electric race-car track on the sparkling kitchen floor and sent his cars screaming around it for an hour not *three feet* away from June Bug. She didn't pounce like they were turbo-charged mice and chew their wheels off. On and on she slept, and none of the things that usually excited her — brooms or race cars or even the smell of pizza dough rising in the oven — had any effect.

Nicola lay partly on the pillow with June Bug, watching her dog's quiet panting. June Bug seemed to be dashing from dream to dream, her white legs twitching. Now and then soft little barks and whimpers escaped her.

"I think she's sick," Nicola told her mother. "I think we should take her to the vet."

Mina examined June Bug. She stroked her velvety ears.

"She's never slept so long before," Nicola said.

Mina nodded. "It's so peaceful around here."

"What if she dies?" Nicola asked. "What if she dies and goes to hell?"

"There isn't any hell," Mina said.

"Are you sure?" Nicola asked.

"Actually, no. But what a funny thing to say. Why hell?"

"Because she's done so many bad things!"

"She's not going to die. She's going to sleep off whatever bug she has. While she's at it, we're going to have a lovely New Year's Eve with no one fighting about the dog."

Mina was right. The Breams ate do-it-yourself pizza with all the toppings set out. Nicola did herself a cheese and dog pepperoni pizza and left a piece for June Bug, in case she woke up.

She did not.

After pizza, they played rummy. In the middle of the game, Terence snuck away and turned back all the clocks so they could have midnight at ten o'clock, for Jackson's sake.

As the false midnight neared, they put away the cards and set a bowl of cold water in the center of the table. Each of them took a candle. Terence lit his, then touched the flame to Mina's wick. She passed the flame to Jared. It traveled all the way around the table until the five candles glowed.

They took turns tipping them over the bowl so the melting wax dribbled into the cold water and hardened into blobs. By these wax blobs, the Breams predicted what the New Year would bring for each of them.

Jackson's wax blob was flat and round.

Mina said, "Money, Jackson!"

"Pancakes," he insisted.

Jared's was a heart. He pumped his fist. "Yes!"

For Terence, a new car. For Mina, less stress at work. Her blob was sort of wedge-shaped, like a piece of cake.

Nicola's little blob had two wing-like bits sticking out.

"A dove? For peace?" Mina suggested.

"A bird is going to poop on you!" Jackson roared.

At ten o'clock, the Breams counted down the seconds and, cheering, drank a New Year's toast with sparkling apple juice. Except for Jared, who stayed up to play Inferno 2, they all went to bed.

Nicola tossed and turned, still worrying about June Bug. While she was worrying, she remembered something.

Two summers ago, the Breams drove to Nova Scotia

to visit Grammy and Grampy. It was a long, long drive. Nicola took Gravol every morning, crushed and stirred into her yoghurt, or she'd get carsick. The Gravol yoghurt made her sleepy.

Almost as sleepy as June Bug today after she licked out the bowls of beige pudding stuff at Shady Oaks.

And Nicola remembered something else. All the pills lined up on the counter at the nursing station. On a bottle of bright blue pills, an orange sticker was fixed.

Warning: May Cause Drowsiness.

It was almost midnight. Nicola got out of bed, dragged her duvet to the kitchen and curled up on the floor with her dog.

"June Bug?" she whispered. "Was there medicine crushed up in that stuff you ate? Wake up. Please."

June Bug dozed on, looking quite contented, which reassured Nicola.

At any moment the fireworks and pot-banging would start. Nicola went and stood at the living-room window, waiting. The tradition on their street was to welcome the New Year by stepping out on the porch at the exact stroke of midnight with pots and spoons.

But tonight the houses on Nicola's street looked as asleep as June Bug, the heavy blanket of snow drawn right up to their porches. No Christmas lights, no inside lights.

Oddly, all the icicles were hanging at a slant.

After what felt like a long time, Nicola returned to

the kitchen and checked the clock. Ten past midnight. No pot banging. No distant pop and crackle of the fireworks at city hall.

"Happy New Year, June Bug," she whispered.

At the sound of her voice, June Bug sat up and looked at Nicola with such a funny expression on her face.

"What is it, June Bug? What?"

June Bug lunged for her water bowl and lapped it up. Nicola refilled it, and June Bug drank the second bowl. Her tail twirled like a propeller, winding her up.

Off she shot, tearing through the sleeping house, around and around, hours of pent-up June Bug energy released at once.

14

LITTLE BLOODY spots of toilet paper were stuck all over Mr. Milton's hollow cheeks. He smelled like soap.

"Happy New Year," Nicola and Lindsay told him.

Along with the treat container, Nicola had brought three pancakes. Lindsay, a mandarin orange.

The fresh tang of the orange made Mr. Milton's eyes widen in surprise. Lindsay put a segment in his hand, and he immediately lifted it to his mouth.

Gratitude filled his gaze.

Nicola said, "Last night we told our futures in melted wax. My little brother's already came true. We had pancakes for breakfast. Eat everything, Mr. Milton. But that mush stuff? It's got pills crushed in it. If they try to give it to you, don't eat it. And don't swallow the blue pill. Just pretend."

Lindsay nodded and handed him another orange segment.

"I only pretend to eat celery," Nicola told him. "Then I spit it in my napkin and drop it on the floor. June Bug takes care of it."

Mr. Milton looked from Nicola to Lindsay in wonderment.

"I think you'll feel a lot better without those pills. But don't go around yelling about strangers. That's probably why they're giving you those pills. Try to stay calm. Then tomorrow, when you're wide awake, June Bug will show you her tricks. You'll really like it."

What June Bug really seemed to want was one of Mr. Milton's pancakes. She stared at Mr. Milton chewing while Mr. Milton stared at Nicola and Lindsay.

Pierre came in with a pill cup and a glass of water.

The last pancake was still in Mr. Milton's hand. He seemed in a hurry to finish it. It was as though he was worried they would take it from him, the way June Bug gulped down the awful things she found on the ground that she wasn't supposed to eat, like cigarette butts and old chicken bones.

"That's got to taste better than the usual. Right, Mr. Milton?" Pierre said. He turned to the girls. "Except it's against the rules. So don't bring him anything else, okay?"

"Okay," Nicola said.

Nicola watched Pierre feed the pills one by one to Mr. Milton. Mr. Milton's Adam's apple didn't move when he took the blue pill.

Pierre said, "Okay, girls. Mr. Milton needs to nap."

"June Bug wants to do a quick trick before we leave." Nicola took out the treats and got June Bug to Crawl across the bed.

They all laughed, except for Mr. Milton.

"We'll have a good visit tomorrow, right?" Nicola said, patting his speckled hand.

"Do not forget," he gasped, and the blue pill fell out of his mouth into his lap. Nicola plucked it out of the covers and slipped it in her pocket.

"That's his favorite expression," Pierre told them as they filed out. "'Do not forget to entertain strangers.' Maybe he ran a nightclub or something."

※

"Let's look it up," Lindsay said when they were walking away from Shady Oaks.

"What?"

"The thing he keeps saying."

"I have to take June Bug home. We can do it there."

Going to Lindsay's would have been smarter. Lindsay didn't have an older brother. Nicola didn't think of this until they got there.

The girls stood like sentinels behind Jared. Nicola cleared her throat several times. It was pointless. She signaled to Lindsay to stay in the den while she got her mother's cellphone from her purse and called their home number.

In half a ring Jared answered, sounding desperate.

"Hi," Nicola said in a giggly voice.

"Who's this?"

"Don't you know me?"

He bolted out of the den with the phone and tore upstairs to his room, passing Nicola in the hall.

Nicola returned to the den. Lindsay had already taken Jared's place at the computer and was closing Inferno 2.

"I might know you," Jared said, breathing hard from running up the stairs in a way Nicola thought would probably disgust Julie Walters-Chen. "Is it Julie?"

Lindsay typed in *Do not forget to entertain strangers.*

Seeing the number of Google results, Nicola hung up. "Three million four hundred and eighty thousand?"

"There's a second part," Lindsay said.

And both girls read it.

For by doing so, many have entertained angels unawares.

✳

Mina looked up from the giant crossword puzzle when the girls came in the kitchen.

"How did it go with the old folks today?"

"The same," Nicola said. "But Mr. Milton was calmer so we could visit him."

"There's a Mr. Milton?" Mina asked.

"Yes."

She laughed. "Look what I just filled in."

Nicola and Lindsay went over. Nicola's eyes swam

at the sight of the tiny black and white squares filling two whole newspaper pages.

Her mother pointed to a word.

"Milton," Lindsay read.

"Really?" Nicola said. "What's the clue?"

"One thousand and fifteen across." Mina turned over the sheet to find the clue. "'He wrote *Paradise Lost.*'"

Lindsay said, "Mr. Milton is in the crossword puzzle?"

"A different Mr. Milton," Mina said. "A famous writer."

"What's *Paradise Lost*?" Nicola asked.

"A very long poem."

"Maybe we should read it to him," Lindsay said.

"Do we have a copy?" Nicola asked.

"I used to. I studied it a long time ago, in university." Mina stood up and stretched. She took off her reading glasses and rubbed her eyes. "I've been at this puzzle all morning. I'm as addicted as Jared is to that computer game. Let's look in the basement."

Mina found her old university books in a trunk in the storage room. "You'll have to dig through it. Put everything else back. Do you girls want lunch?"

"Can Nicola come to my place?" Lindsay said. "My mom's home."

"Of course!" Mina told Nicola. "Have fun and take my phone and be home by three."

"Wasn't that weird that Mr. Milton was in the cross-word puzzle?" Lindsay said as they lifted the books out of the trunk and set them aside in mildewy stacks. "I shivered when your mom said that. Sometimes when I go to a wedding, I try to imagine what the bride's dress will look like and what kind of flowers will be in her bouquet. Sometimes I'm exactly right. I get that shiver then, too."

Nicola changed the subject. "Poems are good. They're nice to read out loud. Mr. Milton will cheer up and want to see June Bug's tricks. Here it is."

A thick paperback with a red and black cover, all dog-eared and written inside.

"June Bug is page-eared," Nicola said. "Her ears fold down like pages."

When they opened the book, it released a musty long-ago scent. Lindsay drew back, but June Bug stood on her hind legs to sniff it.

Prostration. Climb'st. Darksome.

"Is this even English?" Nicola asked.

Lindsay turned the pages. "*Seraphim, Cherubim, Throne,*" she read, plugging her nose.

"Seraphim?" Nicola said.

She carried the book to the bottom of the basement stairs and shouted up, "Mom! Is this a poem about *angels*?"

✳

Lindsay lived in an old brick apartment with its name in slanting gold writing on the front door: The Sheldon Arms Apartments.

Irene, Lindsay's mother, met them at the door. She had glasses with zebra frames.

"I've heard so much about you," she told Nicola.

Over lunch, which was homemade vegetable soup, Lindsay told Irene about their discovery. "The thing Mr. Milton keeps saying is actually an expression."

"What expression?" Irene asked.

"'Do not forget to entertain strangers, because something something about angels."

"And what does it mean?" Irene asked.

"We don't know," Lindsay said. "But it had over three million results on Google. And then we found out that another Mr. Milton wrote a famous book about angels. Nicola's mom had it. We're going to read it after lunch."

"Lindsay," Irene whispered when the girls were clearing the table. "No box today, right?"

"She already knows about it," Lindsay said. "I told her."

They went to Lindsay's room, which was a lot like Nicola's messy room except for magazine pictures of brides taped all over the walls, and the cardboard refrigerator box that took up most of the floor space.

Lindsay said, "That's my Feel Better Box. Go on in."

Nicola hesitated. She got down on her hands and knees and crawled inside.

"Lying down is better," Lindsay said, so Nicola lay on her back on the sleeping bag that padded the floor of the box.

Taped on the ceiling and walls were more magazine pictures — flowers and sunsets and brides — as well as photographs of people Lindsay probably knew, and her bride drawings.

"Look under the pillow," Lindsay told her.

A bottle of spray cologne. Lindsay told Nicola to spray some around, then close her eyes.

After a minute she asked, "How do you feel? Better?"

"Than what?" Nicola asked.

Lindsay squirmed in and lay beside her. Nicola felt worse.

"Which dress do you like the best?" Lindsay asked of the drawings taped above them. Nicola pointed to one at random.

"I love that one, too! I love the heart neckline."

"I'm never getting married," Nicola said. "I'm going to live alone in a big house with lots and lots of dogs. Can we read the book now?"

"Sure. I'll get it," Lindsay said.

"I don't think I'll be able to read in the box. I'm starting to feel funny."

"That might be the Feeling Better starting."

"I don't think so," Nicola said.

15

———

THE LAST DAY of winter break, Nicola brought gingerbread and salmon cookies to reward June Bug for doing her tricks. She wasn't supposed to bring Mr. Milton food, but if he wanted to try some of June Bug's treats, it would be rude to say no.

Mr. Milton was feeling fine today, Glenda told them when she buzzed them in.

The girls sat side by side on the end of his bed with June Bug between them. Lindsay held the treats out for Mr. Milton, whose hand dipped robotically into the container.

Nicola unfolded the sheet of paper she'd brought.

"We figured out you were interested in angels. Then we found out about this famous book about angels written by another Mr. Milton. But we could hardly read it. So last night my mom told me the story. The part she remembers, anyway. I wrote it down."

June Bug sniffed the paper in Nicola's hand, as though to read the story, too.

"*Once upon a time there were some angels who decid-*

ed they didn't like living in heaven and getting bossed around by God," Nicola read. "They wanted to be the boss of themselves. So they started a war with the other angels. But the good angels won and kicked the bad ones out. The bad ones fell from heaven, and when they hit the very bottom, that became hell. The fallen angels turned into demons who only wanted to get back at the good angels. First they thought of starting another war, but they got a better idea. They decided to visit earth and mess people up."

"How does that get back at the good angels?" Lindsay asked.

Nicola lowered the paper. "I asked that, too. Because angels are on the side of people. The bad angels were actually pretty smart. If someone wanted to hurt me, the best way to do it would be to hurt June Bug. Because I love June Bug so much."

Nicola continued reading. "This was a long long time ago. There were only two people on earth then, Adam and Eve."

Mr. Milton, who had slowly crunched through all the treats in the container, lifted one finger in the air.

"I think he wants to say something," Lindsay said.

Nicola looked up from the page again.

"Entertain strangers," Mr. Milton said.

"Do not forget to entertain strangers," Lindsay recited, "for by doing so some have entertained angels unawares."

Mr. Milton's eyes flew open. For a moment something shone out of them that Nicola recognized. June Bug looked at her like that whenever Nicola shook the treat container. Jackson wore the same expression on Christmas morning. Jared did, too, every time the phone rang.

What shone out of Mr. Milton's eyes was hope.

"But what does it mean, Mr. Milton?" Lindsay asked.

"Here," he said, pointing to the bed. "Here — "

June Bug, who had been waiting patiently for a treat, now realized she wasn't getting one. She decided to have some fun, which was the next best thing to a treat. She snatched the story out of Nicola's hand and leapt to the floor.

"No, June Bug!" Nicola cried. "I'm not finished reading it!"

Nicola made a grab for June Bug, who scooted under the bed. On her hands and knees, Nicola peered at her dog gleefully tearing the story to bits.

"Bad!" Nicola said. "Bad, bad June Bug!"

✳

Really, until then, June Bug hadn't been so bad. She'd scratched under some doors. She'd bitten Pierre's nose. She'd licked out the mush bowls. Other than that, she'd almost been good.

And so Nicola had almost forgotten about June Bug's One More Chance.

Until that night.

After dinner, Nicola took a bath. Her parents made her, because of school the next day.

What Nicola liked about taking a bath was how June Bug would sit patiently on the mat, waiting for her to step dripping from the tub. Then she would spring up and lovingly lick the water off Nicola's legs with her tickly pink tongue.

What Nicola hated was leaving her wet hair down. Poor June Bug had no braid to chew until the next day. And her brothers always teased her.

"Ratpunzel, Ratpunzel, let down your hair!" Jackson sang.

"It's RA-punzel," Nicola screeched.

Jared said, "Oh, Lady Godiva. Where's your horse?"

Lady Godiva was a lady in a story who rode naked on a horse with only her long hair covering her private parts.

"Mo-o-o-o-m!" Nicola wailed.

Mina was working on her crossword puzzle in the den. She glanced up, her eyes red from squinting at the tiny numbered boxes.

"Stop it, you two. Leave your sister alone."

In pajamas, wet hair in a towel turban, Nicola fled to the kitchen where she poured herself a bowl of cereal. She remembered how hungrily Mr. Milton had crunched June Bug's treats. Did anyone in Shady Oaks Retirement Home get a snack before bed? Probably not.

Then a familiar cry rang out. "June Bug! Oh, June Bug! No!"

Nicola raced back to the den where June Bug was merrily shredding a section of the newspaper the way she'd shredded Nicola's story that afternoon. Mina stood gaping.

"No! June Bug!" Nicola cried. "That's Mom's puzzle!"

Jared, at the computer, swiveled in his chair to watch.

"Mom, I'm sorry!" Nicola cried. "I'll tape it back together. June Bug, stop!"

Nicola caught a corner of the paper. June Bug pulled back, growling. She sounded fierce, like she was prepared to rip off Nicola's arm to keep the paper.

"There's Chance Number Three!" Jared hooted. "One, Two, Three! That dog is out of here!"

Nicola sank to the floor, sobbing. June Bug forgot the crossword puzzle and clamped onto the corner of the towel instead, tugging until she managed to pull it off Nicola's head. Gleefully, she pranced out of the room dragging the towel.

Jared kept chanting, "One, Two, Three! One, Two, Three!"

"Stop it," Mina told him. "You, too, Nicola. It's time for bed."

Still weeping, Nicola collected the scraps of puzzle. Jared put his foot over one. Unable to pry it off, she crawled under the desk and flicked the switch on the power bar.

"Hey!" Jared roared. "I was in the Seventh Circle! Now I'm back to the Sixth!"

Nicola ran with all the pieces gathered in her pajama top. She found her mother in her bedroom with June Bug, trying to make her give up the towel. Nicola took the treat container off the shelf and shook it.

June Bug let go of the towel. She Sat and Waved.

And Mina laughed.

"I'm sorry, Mom. Please don't send her away. Please don't let that be her Last Chance."

Mina pulled Nicola close. "Nicola, we would never send June Bug away. We love her. You were the one who came up with the idea of the Three Chances."

"I was?"

"Yes."

"Because Dad said it wasn't working out. He said he'd take her to the SPCA if she was bad."

"He was frustrated, Nicola. Getting a dog hasn't been the easiest thing we've done as a family. Frankly, having Jackson was easier."

Mina shook a treat into her hand and held it out to June Bug. "I was supposed to be relaxing over the holidays. Instead I spent all day running to the computer. Running to the dictionary. Twice I woke up in the middle of the night with a crossword answer. I went downstairs to fill it in then couldn't get back to sleep. It was worse than work."

"So June Bug did a good deed?" Nicola asked.

"I'd say so." Mina turned to the little black-and-white dog still waving one paw in the air. "Thank you, June Bug. I'm free at last."

16

————

THAT NIGHT Nicola slept peacefully — a long dreamless sleep that left her feeling so light in the morning, it seemed she'd grown wings. Because June Bug was safe. She wouldn't ever be sent to the SPCA despite all the bad things she did.

At school Ms. Phibbs had changed the seating. Now Lindsay sat all the way on the other side of the room.

She waved her hand in the air. "Ms. Phibbs? Excuse me? Can I still sit beside Nicola? Please?"

Ms. Phibbs looked up from her lesson book, her eyes a little bloodshot, the sides of her nose chapped.

"Why?"

"We're friends," Lindsay said.

Nicola glanced over at Lindsay, no longer the girl who sat next to her chattering away about brides. Nicola was grateful Lindsay had helped her over the holidays, but she wasn't sure she wanted to hang around with her at school.

"I'm okay here," Nicola said.

"There's your answer," Ms. Phibbs said. "No."

Lindsay stared at Nicola, her hurt eyes framed in pink. When she turned away, the airy feeling began to seep out of Nicola. A heavy feeling replaced it. A sinking feeling that weighed her down in her chair and caused her to tilt slightly to the left.

Ms. Phibbs called out names. If she called you, you had to write a homework answer on the board. Last year they corrected their homework in groups, but this year they did it in this boring way. Meanwhile, a bad taste filled Nicola's mouth.

She looked around at the new classroom arrangement. There was a wide aisle not quite down the middle of the room. It was a split class, but the aisle didn't separate the two grades. Some other logic had placed Gavin Heinrichs, who threw the Murder Ball so savagely, on the same side as Margo Tamm, who was known to "accidentally" bump and kick people and when they said, "Ouch," reply, "Do you think I care how you feel?"

Nicola was on their side, not Lindsay's.

At lunch Lindsay found Nicola, who was more or less hiding from her in the crowd of kids milling in the cold around the cordoned-off playground equipment.

Lindsay said, "Are we visiting Shady Oaks today?"

"Actually, June Bug doesn't need to go anymore because my mom promised they'd never send her to the SPCA."

"Oh," Lindsay said, squinching so the pink glasses

rose and fell on her face. "What about her going to hell?"

"There's no such place."

"Are you sure about that?"

Mina had answered this same question. She'd said she wasn't sure. So had Ignacio, back in the fall. The horrible taste welled up in Nicola's mouth again and made her feel like spitting.

"And what about Mr. Milton and the others?" Lindsay asked.

"I was only going for my dog."

Nicola felt miserable the whole rest of the day.

Lindsay spoke to her one more time at the end of school, after the class had finished their detention for not doing a page of homework that Ms. Phibbs hadn't even assigned. The girls were in the cloakroom where their coat hooks were still side by side.

Lindsay whispered, "Why is Ms. Phibbs so mean?"

She seemed to have brushed off Nicola's rejection. Nicola was relieved.

"I had Ms. Phibbs last year and she wasn't mean at all."

Lindsay said, "I bet she's getting divorced."

"Why would you say that?"

"Because that's what happens when you get a divorce. You feel really, really sad."

"She doesn't seem sad," Nicola said. "She seems mad."

"You feel sad and mad."

They went downstairs and out the door of the school.

"What are you doing now?" Nicola asked.

"Going to Shady Oaks." And Lindsay turned and walked off, leaving Nicola standing in the cold until her eyelashes stuck together.

⁕

They had library time during school to work on their wildlife PowerPoint presentations, but not nearly enough. That night Nicola had to ask her mother to make Jared get off the computer. He slumped on the couch in the den doing his own homework, announcing every few minutes how much time she had left.

"Twelve minutes."

Coyotes, like all dogs, can hear sounds from four times as far away as humans, Nicola typed.

"Ten minutes."

Coyotes can detect smells at a concentration 100 million times lower than humans.

When her thirty minutes were over, Jared muscled her off the chair.

"I have to save it!" Nicola shrieked.

Then she stood behind him watching him play.

"You said there were nine kinds of angels."

Jared rattled them off. "Seraphim, Cherubim, Thrones, Dominions, Virtues, Powers, Principalities, Archangels, Angels. They all have special powers. Seraphim blow fire. I'm on the Principalities now. They join with other Principalities to form armies."

"But not in real life, right? In the game?"

He pounded the keys, ignoring her. "Die! Die! Yes! Here we go!"

On the screen the game opened into something different. One of the flaming blobs crashed down in a rocky ravine. Once the smoke cleared, Nicola saw that the blob had become a creature with horrible charred bat wings. It got to its feet and loped choppily away.

"See what he's doing?" Jared asked.

Lifting its hand to its blackened face.

"He's covering his nose. Because it stinks in the Seventh Circle. See the steaming piles everywhere? No one poops and scoops in hell."

"Is this hell?" Nicola asked.

"It's the First Ring of the Seventh Circle, where the violent are condemned."

"I guess that's where you're going," Nicola said.

"I hope so. It's my favorite circle so far. You should see where the annoying people end up. I don't think you're going to be too comfortable there."

A monster reared up from behind a boulder, giving Nicola a start. It had a hairy body even more muscley than Pierre's, a bull's horned head and red glowing eyes. A double-headed ax was slung over its massive shoulder.

The black angel and the monster began to fight.

Nicola turned away. "There aren't any dogs in hell, are there?"

"In the Third Circle. A three-headed dog. You're not leaving? You have to see the boiling river of blood."

How could Jared sleep after that? In bed, every time Nicola closed her eyes, she saw that murky underground place, its sunless sky. She saw swarming flies and dueling monsters. The boiling river of blood, she imagined.

When she couldn't stand it any longer, she dragged her duvet to where there was someone who would keep her safe and warm. Someone small and black and white.

Much later, the kitchen light flicked on.

"Nicola?" Terence said.

Nicola sat up blinking. The tears came right away. "I can't sleep!"

Terence, in a T-shirt and boxer shorts, got down on the kitchen floor. He pulled Nicola's duvet over his bare legs. June Bug wriggled between them and sighed.

"What's bothering you?" he asked.

"Jared showed me Inferno 2! It was horrible! Is there such a place as hell?"

"Yes," Terence said, and Nicola collapsed into him and sobbed.

"But it's not like that game. That game is a metaphor."

"What's that?"

"A way of explaining something to make it easier to understand. What happened in the game?"

"An angel fell from heaven and landed in hell. Jared said that was where the violent people went. Then the horriblest monster appeared with a horrible ax thing. And I didn't even wait to see the boiling river of blood."

"You see? In the game, violence punishes violent people. In real life, violent people are tormented by their violent thoughts. And if they're not too terrible, if they actually feel bad about the things they think and do, they're tormented by their conscience."

"They feel guilty."

"Yes. There's no actual place called hell. It's here." He tapped her head. "Does that make sense?"

"Sort of." Nicola sniffed.

"Is there any gingerbread left?"

"No."

"So there's another hell," Terence said, smiling.

"There's more than one?"

"There are many. Mine, at this particular moment, is waking up in the middle of the night with a powerful yearning for my daughter's gingerbread, only to discover there isn't any left. I guess I'll have cereal. Do you want some?"

Nicola said no. "I'm going back to bed. Thanks, Dad."

She kissed him goodnight. And she kissed her little dog, who had slept right through this Comforting Talk about What Hell Really Is.

17

———

AT SCHOOL THE next day, Margot Tamm tripped Nicola so she nearly fell on her face in the wide aisle that separated the two sides of the classroom. This happened when Nicola was returning to her desk after asking Lindsay if she'd visited Shady Oaks the day before. Lindsay had pushed up her pink glasses and made a shooing motion with her hand. Either she didn't want to talk just then, or she never wanted to speak to Nicola again.

Nicola laid her forehead on the cool top of her desk. She was the one who had announced in front of the whole class that she didn't want to sit with Lindsay. Why? Lindsay wasn't so bad. Even though she wore pink glasses and was always talking about brides, she wasn't really a clothes-and-hair girl. So why had Nicola been mean to her in front of everyone?

The bad way she had treated Lindsay was becoming a feeling, a monstrous feeling. A feeling with horns.

Nicola lifted her head off the desk and narrowed her eyes at Margo Tamm one seat ahead, all gussied up with hair thingies. With her finger and thumb Nicola flicked Margo's shoulder as hard as she could. When Margo squealed and swung around, Nicola hissed, "Do you think I care how you feel?"

Ms. Phibbs acted like she didn't see. These little skirmishes were always breaking out on the left side of the room right under her nose. But now Gavin Heinrichs swaggered to the front to give his presentation on sasquatches.

A sasquatch was hairy. It had a weightlifter's body. All it was missing were the horns. Nicola folded over her desk and waited for Gavin to finish. Then everyone had to clap and ask a question. Even Nicola, who had plugged her ears for the whole presentation.

"But are there really sasquatches?" she asked.

"Yes!" Gavin said. "You saw the picture."

"It was all blurry. It could have been a bear or a man in a costume or — "

"Next question?" Ms. Phibbs said.

※

When she got home, Nicola phoned Lindsay.

"I'm sorry," she said. "Sorry for saying that I didn't want to sit beside you."

"Why did you say it?" Lindsay asked. "Did you only want to be my friend for the holidays?"

"No. School's just so awful now. Everyone's so mean.

I said a mean thing without really thinking about it. Last night, I could hardly sleep."

Only then did Nicola's monstrous feeling lumber back to the dark place it lived.

Lindsay sniffed on her end of the line.

"Did you go to Shady Oaks?" Nicola asked.

"Why do you want to know?"

"I'm wondering what happened."

"So you weren't only going for June Bug?" Lindsay asked.

"I was at the beginning. Now I'm worried about them."

Finally, she sounded like the old bubbly Lindsay. "I knew it! I knew you cared!"

"Is Mr. Milton taking the pills?"

"No. He was wide awake and walking around. But he's still talking about entertaining strangers. I think Jorie's wrong, though."

"About what?" Nicola asked.

"I have to hang up in a second. I'm going to the library with Ignacio."

"What's Jorie wrong about?"

"I don't think Mr. Milton is saying the same thing over and over because he had a stroke. He brought me to Mr. Fitzpatrick's door and said, 'Do not forget.' And he did the same at Mrs. Michaels' door. And Mrs. Tanaka's. Their doors are locked. I don't like that. It's like a prison. And, Nicola?"

"What?"

"Outside each door, he pointed to his eye. I think he saw something. He's trying to tell us about it. Remember what he said the first time we came?"

"He asked if we were strangers."

"And he said to *get them out*. Ignacio's here. I have to go now. I'll see you tomorrow."

18

FOR HER wildlife presentation, Lindsay dressed up in a ruffled white top. Nicola could almost see rays of excitement beaming off her. She looked like a person who had just won the lottery. A person who knew some important secret she was bursting to tell.

Her title page came up on the screen: *Angels*. The picture was vaguely familiar to Nicola. A stained-glass angel holding a scroll.

The golden-haired angel from the window at Our Lady of Perpetual Help Church.

"Huh?" someone said. Probably Gavin Heinrichs or Margo Tamm.

Appearance, Food, Habitat, Life Cycle and Communication were the categories Ms. Phibbs had assigned.

Lindsay flipped quickly through a series of slides. Snow angels. Cupids from valentine cards. A statue on a gravestone. But most of the pictures were paintings and sculptures showing angels. Babies and adults, male and female. Some were dressed colorfully, with gold pointed hats. Others were all in white. One held a dove, another a sword. Some had halos, but each halo was different — a sort of plate stuck to the back of the head, or spiky rays, or an aura of light.

"So, Appearance," Lindsay said. "I just showed you so many different ways angels might appear, but the truth is that they don't actually have bodies."

"Huh?" Again.

"They take on other forms, like human or animal. Something we'll recognize. So how can you tell a person from an angel? Because they give off a sweet perfume. But people might wear perfume and aftershave, right? So how do you tell? Because they glow!"

Lindsay clicked on another slide. A gold X-ray of an angel, an angel made entirely of light.

Some kids were whispering to each other. From the left side of the room, scoffing laughter.

"Okay, Food," Lindsay said. "This is easy!"

There was one sentence on the screen: *They don't eat!*

"For Habitat, angels can live anywhere. They're found all over the world, in every culture. But they prefer to be near people. Because they exist to help people."

She clicked through a series of pictures that showed a country on a map, a photograph of the place, then an angel. Thailand. India. Canada. Italy. Russia.

As the whispers grew louder, Lindsay sped up. "Life Cycle. Easy again! *They don't die!*" she read. "Communication. This is so amazing."

They sing instead of speak.

From the left side of the room, Margo Tamm screeched like an opera singer.

Lindsay reddened, adding, "To communicate with humans, they leave signs that most of the time we don't even notice. Because we're not looking for them."

She scrunched her nose so her glasses lifted, as though she was wondering whether to say the next thing.

"But the thing I like best about angels is that in so many of the pictures they look like they're wearing wedding dresses."

Her last slide showed a Christmas card angel in a long white gown.

"Thank you," she said, taking a bow.

Ms. Phibbs, sitting at her desk, squeezed the bridge of her nose. "Lindsay? The assignment was about animals. You told me you were presenting on squirrels."

"I was going to. I love squirrels! But yesterday I got these really interesting books on angels for a friend. I stayed up until eleven o'clock redoing everything."

"But angels aren't animals, are they?" Ms. Phibbs said. "They're not even real."

"Gavin did sasquatches."

"Sasquatches are real!" Gavin Heinrichs bellowed.

Ms. Phibbs' lips tightened and she crossed her arms. Nicola could see the lumpy place in the sleeve of her cardigan where she tucked her tissues. "Questions?"

Nicola put up her hand. "What kind of signs do they leave?"

"It could be like a word in a crossword puzzle."

Inside Nicola a funny feeling started up. A fluttery, butterflies-in-the-tummy feeling.

"Do you have a source for that?" Ms. Phibbs asked Lindsay, because they were supposed to list where they found their facts.

"I used the Internet. And the two library books I took out for my friend."

"Have you ever seen an angel?" asked Aleisha Durmaz, who sat on Lindsay's side of the room.

"I think so," Lindsay said. "I might have seen three of them. Maybe more. I wasn't looking before. I didn't know to look. You might have seen one, too. They're really common, actually."

"Lindsay, I'm going to stop you here," Ms. Phibbs said. "We don't discuss religion at school out of respect for other faiths."

"But all religions have angels, Ms. Phibbs," Lindsay said. "Christians, Muslims, Buddhists, Hindus and Jews. I showed you some of them."

"This is getting silly. You may sit down."

Lindsay shuffled back to her desk with everyone staring at her instead of applauding like Ms. Phibbs had made them do for the other presenters. After a few minutes of not opening her math book, she raised her hand and asked to go to the bathroom. Ms. Phibbs said she could.

Lindsay was gone a long time. Eventually, Nicola put

up her hand and asked to go, too. Ms. Phibbs seemed to have forgotten about Lindsay because she gave Nicola permission even though this year's rule was that only one person could leave the room at a time.

Nicola looked for Lindsay in the bathrooms on all three floors of Queen Elizabeth Elementary, but didn't find her.

✳

When school was over, Nicola walked to the Sheldon Arms Apartments. Lindsay buzzed her in. Nicola climbed the stairs and found the apartment door open. She shed her boots and coat and went straight to Lindsay's room, where two blue socks jutted from the Feel Better Box.

"Why did you leave school?" Nicola asked.

"Ms. Phibbs said my report wasn't respectful, but she was the disrespectful one. It made me mad. I'm okay now, though. Come in."

Nicola crawled into the box where the cologne smell was thick. She lay down next to Lindsay so they were squashed together.

"What did you mean about the crossword puzzle?"

Lindsay said, "Couldn't it be a sign?"

"It was just a coincidence."

"But remember that flowery smell at Shady Oaks? The good smell around Mr. Fitzpatrick and Mrs.

Michaels and Mrs. Tanaka? A sweet perfume is a sign that an angel is nearby. I have a source for that. Do you want to see the books?"

Nicola felt that fluttering again. She closed her eyes. When she opened them, she was looking right at a picture of Irene taped above her head.

"That's your mom," she said.

Irene in a wedding dress. The picture was cut in half.

"Doesn't she look beautiful?" Lindsay asked. "Doesn't she look happy?"

"Where's the other half of the picture?"

"They got divorced. Do you want to see the dress?" Lindsay asked.

Anything to get out of the box.

In the hall, Lindsay opened a cupboard and climbed the shelves of sheets and towels. She pulled down a white garbage bag and lifted out the dress.

"It's really pretty," Nicola said. And it was. The sleeves were puffed at the shoulders, the bodice stiff with tiny pearls.

"Can you think of anything else you only wear once? That's why a wedding dress is so special. Because you only wear it once and no matter what happens after that, you're always happy the day you wear it." Lindsay rolled up the dress and stuffed it back in the bag.

Nicola asked, "Is your mom unhappy?"

"She was. Mostly she's stressed now."

They returned to Lindsay's room. Nicola hesitated in the doorway.

"We don't have to go back in the box," Lindsay said. "I already feel better. I feel better because you came over."

"Lindsay," Nicola said. "You don't really think there are angels at Shady Oaks."

"That's what Mr. Milton thinks. That's what he was trying to tell me. And when June Bug put on her show? I felt like something really special happened and it wasn't June Bug doing her tricks."

"I felt it, too," Nicola said.

"It was because *they* were there. Mrs. Michaels and Mr. Fitzpatrick and Mrs. Tanaka."

19

———

FIRST THEY stopped at Feeler's Flowers, around the corner from the apartment in a strip mall between a Chinese restaurant and a dollar store. A flower shop was a much nicer place to work than a lawyer's office or the computing center at the college where Nicola's father spent every day. Nicola told Irene this.

"You're right," Irene said as she unpacked a box of greeting cards. "It would be heavenly, if only I sold some flowers." She looked closely at Lindsay. "Feeling better, Ms. Feeler?"

Lindsay nodded. "We're going to walk June Bug."

"You know it's already four? It'll be dark in an hour."

"I'll be back by then," Lindsay said, with a hug for Irene.

As soon as they left the shop, Nicola told Lindsay, "It smells good in there. It smells sweet. So is an angel nearby?"

"Maybe," Lindsay said. "Or maybe it's just the flowers. We don't know, right?"

"Every single flower shop can't have angels in it," Nicola said.

"Why not?"

"There are flower shops everywhere. Flowers are everywhere."

"Angels are everywhere."

Nicola sighed.

They picked up June Bug, then set out again. Not to visit Shady Oaks, but to see if Lindsay was right. If the doors to Mrs. Michaels', Mr. Fitzpatrick's and Mrs. Tanaka's rooms were locked, Lindsay and Nicola would have to look in at them from the outside.

"I hope the curtains aren't closed," Nicola said.

"There aren't any. At least, there weren't in Mr. Milton's room."

"No smiling. No laughing. No curtains," Nicola said.

Two blocks from Shady Oaks the little dog figured out where they were going and began pulling so hard on the leash that Nicola had to carry her.

"We haven't visited for a few days. She really wants to go back."

When they reached Shady Oaks, they saw the fence. Next door was a house. These Shady Oaks neighbors had young children. Nicola spotted the roof of a plastic playhouse protruding from a snowy hump, right next to the fence.

Nicola climbed up first and looked over into the yard of Shady Oaks. A tamped-down path led from the back gate to the back door, probably made by the people who delivered the food. Slanted icicles hung from the eaves and over the high windows, as thick as bars.

Lindsay passed June Bug up to Nicola and the two of them jumped down into the untouched snow on the Shady Oaks side. Lindsay went next. She waded to the corner of the building where the garbage and recycling bins stood and dragged one back. Clambering up on it, she broke off an icicle and used it to knock the others down.

Now she was just tall enough to see in the window. One peek and she jumped to the ground, making a face.

"What?" Nicola asked.

Lindsay pointed to the window.

Nicola climbed up on the bin and looked in herself. She saw a room eerily lit from the blue glow of a computer screen. Then she noticed another light across the room.

A cigarette.

A man was stretched out on a sofa, one arm bent to form a pillow behind his head. The man Nicola had seen the first day she came to Shady Oaks. He was smoking, flicking the ash into an ashtray balanced on his chest. When he lifted the cigarette to his mouth and sucked on it, the end flared red and reflected in his glasses lenses.

Nicola shuddered.

After a few puffs, he butted the cigarette and stood up, tall and hulking. He crossed to the sleeping computer and pressed a button.

Instantly, a murky cartoon landscape bloomed across the monitor, teeming with flies.

"Uggh!" Nicola said, jumping down from the bin.

"Mr. Devon?" Lindsay asked.

"He's playing Inferno 2!"

Above them, a fingernail of moon hung in a graying sky. It was getting dark.

June Bug had already moved on to the next window. She stood on her hind legs with her front paws on the wall, sniffing the air and wagging like a maniac.

"We should hurry," Nicola said, pulling the bin over. She got Lindsay to hold June Bug back while she swatted at the icicles.

"Whose room is it?" Lindsay asked.

Mrs. Tanaka's. Nicola shouldn't have been able to tell. She shouldn't have been able to see Mrs. Tanaka shut up like this in the dark.

But she could. She blinked a few times, pressing her forehead and mittens to the frosty window.

The glass was vibrating. The vibration became tingles, the tingles a feeling spreading through her.

That feeling she'd had before.

"What?" Lindsay asked when Nicola climbed down.

The look on Nicola's face must have said it all. Lindsay clambered up on the bin and, looking in, gasped. Gasped, then whooped and leapt down into the snow bank.

Lindsay hugged Nicola and tried to dance her around,

but in their cumbersome winter clothes Nicola stumbled and fell into the thick snow. She moved her arms and legs around, swishing out an angel.

June Bug jumped onto her chest and licked inside her ears and nose and on the frozen apples of her cheeks.

The two of them, girl and dog, sprawled, kissing and giggling in ecstasy over what the girls had seen and the little dog had smelled.

20

"LINDSAY'S MOTHER phoned here, very worried. She said Lindsay had promised to be home by five, but it's quarter to six and completely dark. Then I was worried."

"I'm sorry," Nicola said, sitting across from Mina at the kitchen table with folded hands.

They had a Talk, only this time Nicola did the talking. She explained all the awful things that went on at Shady Oaks, how the food was so bad and how there was nothing to do.

"And so many rules! Anything that would make the place nicer, there's a rule against it. Also, there aren't enough nurses. They're overworked and it makes some of them grumpy."

Mina said, "Sadly, Nicola, that sounds like a lot of those places. Someone at work? Her mother was in a home. She said it was hell."

"Hell the metaphor?" Nicola asked.

"What?"

"Dad said hell was a metaphor, but I'm starting to think it's a real place, too."

Jared came in the kitchen. June Bug lifted her head off her pillow and wagged, even though he hated her.

"When's dinner?"

"It's going to be late. Your sister needs to figure out her Consequences."

"How about the guillotine? Where's Dad?"

"At swimming lessons with Jackson. Order pizza."

Jared pumped his fist. "Yes!"

"And they give them pills that make them sleep all day," Nicola said. "Or mix it in their food."

"Are you sure? Old people sleep a lot."

"They lock them in their rooms."

"If they have dementia, they may wander, Nicola. You can't have those folks escaping in this climate. They wouldn't last ten minutes."

"Escaping?" Nicola said.

"So what are your Consequences going to be for not coming home when you're supposed to?"

"Maybe we should write a letter to the government and tell them how bad the place is. That's what Lindsay wants to do."

"Good idea," Mina said, getting up from the table. "You two can do that on Monday. But this weekend, you're grounded. And no Shady Oaks."

✳

Since she couldn't tell her mother, she told her dog as they lay together on Nicola's bed.

"Mrs. Tanaka's room was dark. They leave them like that. Isn't it awful? Except it wasn't dark. It wasn't dark because, June Bug? This is the amazing part. *Mrs. Tanaka makes her own light.*"

June Bug repositioned Nicola's braid between her paws and chewed with gusto.

"It was a soft and silvery sort of light shining off her face. This part I'm sure about — the most beautiful feeling came over me when I saw her."

June Bug tilted her head to the side. It was so cute the way that line divided her face down the middle, black on one side, the other white.

※

Nicola spent most of her weekend of Consequences in her room with June Bug, reading the books Lindsay had loaned her.

"What is an angel, June Bug? Good question. It's a being of pure spirit. Do angels have bodies? No. But they *can assume bodily form*. That means they appear to us like they do have bodies. In this book?"

Nicola lifted it so June Bug could see which one she meant. June Bug sniffed it.

"This book is full of stories about people who say they've been helped by angels. Mostly they leave signs to communicate with us. To each other, they sing. Sometimes they do seem to speak. Listen to this."

Nicola found the passage. "*However their language sounds or seems, it is actually a direct communication into our minds.* That's like how you communicate with me. Sometimes you just look at me and I know what you mean."

June Bug rolled over, wriggling and snorting on her back, communicating directly to Nicola that she was happy.

The most important thing Nicola read was that angels loved people. The books, combined with the beautiful and mysterious sight of Mrs. Tanaka glowing in her bed, made Nicola feel as if she, too, were glowing from the inside.

Sunday morning, getting ready to walk June Bug, she paused at the long window beside the front door, a window she had looked through a thousand times before. The pane was coated with ice, a feathery frost-drawn picture of what the world would look like if she could see it the way it truly was.

The sky traced with wings.

21

——

To: Patient Quality Care Office
From: Nicola Bream and Lindsay Feeler
Priority: HIGH!!

We are two grade five girls who have been visiting Shady Oaks Retirement Home. We're writing
you now to complain about how the old people are
treated there. The food is really terrible and nobody
wants to eat it. There are no fun things to do and
no decorations for Christmas or Hanukkah. Flowers
aren't even allowed! And the old people are given
sleeping pills in the day. Some are locked in their
rooms. Will you please investigate and do something
about this place as soon as possible? The patients
should be smiling and laughing and not sleeping all
the time. Also, one bath every month? How would
you like that?

   Please help them!
   Nicola Bream and Lindsay Feeler

✳

"This is what we know," Nicola said, lying on the bed with June Bug while Lindsay sat at the foot. "Mr. Milton went into one of their rooms. Mrs. Tanaka's, or Mr. Fitzpatrick's, or Mrs. Michaels'. Or maybe all of them. He saw something that surprised him so much that he started to talk again. Now he's trying to get someone to let them out."

"We know they're angels," said Lindsay.

"Mrs. Tanaka seemed to glow," Nicola agreed. "But why didn't we notice before?"

"Because the lights are so bright! And here's another thing about Shady Oaks. The TV is always blaring. Couldn't that be to drown out the sound of their singing?"

"I wonder about that Mr. Devon," Nicola said. "I really do."

"He gave me the creeps!"

June Bug stretched her muzzle along Nicola's thigh and sighed. Her white ear was turned inside out. Nicola flipped it back. "Say they *are* angels. What are they even doing there?"

Lindsay's face scrunched up. "They give off light, which we really need in winter, right?"

"Hey!" Nicola said. "Did you notice? Hardly anyone put up lights this year?"

Lindsay frowned. "I wondered why it didn't seem

like a Christmassy Christmas. The lights are one of the nicest things."

"There are all these holidays with lights. Hanukkah. Diwali," Nicola said. "New Year's Eve fireworks. Except there weren't any fireworks this year, either."

"So do they glow to put more light in the world?" Lindsay asked.

"Jackson has to have a night light," Nicola said. "But what about this? When someone's smart, we say they're bright. Or brilliant. So maybe they glow to remind us to be smarter. To use our heads and think."

"Ah!" Lindsay said, looking out the window. "I have to get home before dark. I should go."

Nicola and June Bug walked her to the door. "I like talking about these things," she told Lindsay. "It makes me believe in them a little bit more."

"I totally believe in them," said Lindsay.

"What I need," Nicola told Lindsay, "is a sign."

22

―――

FOR A FLORIST, Valentine's Day starts at the end of January. Irene was decorating Feeler's Flowers and Lindsay asked Nicola if she wanted to help. For the next few days Nicola raced home after school to walk June Bug, then raced over to the shop.

The girls came up with good ideas, not just about decorating. One was to sell valentines, too, not just the little cards tucked in bouquets.

"Like, for kids."

"That's a great idea," Irene said. "But it's a bit late to order them."

Lindsay took twenty dollars from the cash register. The girls marched next door to the dollar store and bought eighteen boxes of valentines. They used one box for decorating, stringing the valentines in the window with red and pink ribbon. Irene had rolls of every color ribbon in the back room where her workbench was.

"There's something else I don't understand about

140

angels," Nicola told Lindsay as they worked. "They want to help people, right?"

"If you ask for help, it will come," Lindsay said. "You read that, right? Sometimes you don't realize you've been helped. Like when my mom and dad got divorced. I really wanted them to stay together because my mom was sad. And mad. But we moved and she bought the shop. Now, even though she's stressed about money, she's happier than she ever was. So the angels did help us. It just wasn't what I expected."

"You asked angels to help you?" Nicola asked.

"Not exactly. I didn't know I could! But that's the wonderful thing about them. Hoping for something is the same as asking them for help."

Nicola was hole-punching the valentines. She brushed the confetti into the greens bin.

"Oh, save that!" Lindsay said. "I can throw it at the next wedding."

"You're the craziest friend I've ever had," Nicola said, and Lindsay laughed.

"Okay," Nicola went on. "Suppose what you say is true. Then why doesn't Mr. Milton ask the angels for help? They're all locked in together in Shady Oaks. And why don't the angels help each other? Or themselves?"

✳

The next day Lindsay thought of candy.

"Boxes of chocolates," she told Irene. "It would be convenient if people could get their flowers and chocolates in the same place on Valentine's Day."

"And," Nicola said, "you should offer dog treats!"

She explained how the world was divided. There were places that welcomed dogs, and those that didn't. Banks, yes. Bookstores, yes. Libraries, no. Grocery stores, no. It made no sense.

"June Bug pulls all the way to the bank because she knows she'll get a treat there."

The next day Lindsay brought her 100 gel pens and she and Nicola made a DOGS WELCOME sign for the door of the shop.

Nicola got another idea when she looked into the greens bin. The flowers in the bin were too open to sell, or their leaves were tinged brown, but they were still nice. The girls pulled the petals off and scattered them on the sidewalk outside the shop, a pink and red and yellow carpet advertising what was inside.

Looking at them reminded Nicola of her first visit to Our Lady of Perpetual Help. How, tripping up the aisle to confess for June Bug, she had followed a flower petal trail. She'd assumed they'd fallen off the bride's bouquet.

All week they checked their email — Nicola in the morning before Jared got up, then later, with Lindsay, on the computer in the shop.

No reply came to their two-exclamation-point, High Priority letter.

On Friday, when they went back to Shady Oaks, Glenda was at the nursing station. She looked crosser than ever, like her ponytail was pulled too tight. She pointed silently to the unsilent lounge where the Shopping Channel was advertising Thermadore Thumbless Texting Mittens at full volume.

"Is Mr. Milton in his room?" the girls asked.

Glenda's face closed up. On the counter behind her was a box of tissues. She plucked one out, then stood for a minute with her back turned.

Crying?

She pulled herself together and turned around. "He's gone."

"Really?" Nicola grinned. "Someone from the Patient Quality Care Office came?"

"The ambulance," Glenda answered. "Two nights ago. It was too late."

23

———

"Sweetheart," Mina told Nicola that night. "I know it's sad. But it had nothing to do with you. It wasn't your fault."

"Yes, it was!"

And now that Nicola had finally lifted her face out of the pillow, June Bug began kissing away her tears and snot. Nicola pushed her off.

"I should have written a letter the first day I went to Shady Oaks! Then they would have come in time to save him!"

"Who?"

"The Patient Quality Care Office!"

"Nicola, even if you had written them earlier, it can take ages and ages for anything to happen. Years, sometimes."

"Years?"

Mina nodded. "And, sweetheart? The people at Shady Oaks? They're old. They're at the end of their lives. You cheered up Mr. Milton in his last days. You did a good deed. We're proud of you."

It wasn't good enough. Not with the others still locked in there.

"Do you believe in angels, Mom?"

"In actual angels? No. But I believe in being good and helping others. Every time you do that, you're an angel."

Nicola sat up cross-legged and flung back her braid. "You mean *I* could be an angel?"

"I think you already are one," Mina said, gathering Nicola in her arms for a hug.

All at once Nicola understood why Mr. Milton kept asking if she was a stranger. If you entertained strangers, some of them might turn out to be angels. He was asking if Nicola was an angel come to help.

"Angels give off a sweet perfume when they're near," Nicola said.

"You would too if you'd take a bath more often. Did you learn that in those books you were reading?"

"And from Lindsay. She did her project on angels. They leave signs for us to find so we know they're there. Most of the time, though, we don't notice the signs."

"What kind of signs?" Mina asked.

"Like when I found Shady Oaks. I found it because someone had made a snow angel out front. That could be a sign, right?"

Mina half-nodded. "I guess it could. It would be lovely if it was."

"I keep wanting just one more sign." Nicola stroked

the little dog in her lap. "I have to keep my eyes open. And I have to use my head. That's what they want us to do. That's why they glow."

Terence tapped on the open door. He had Jackson by the hand. "Someone wants to say goodnight."

Jackson came in and hugged Nicola, which he hadn't done for a long time. It felt good. Her father did the same, like every night. He said he was sorry for her loss.

And Mina smiled. "You could be an angel now, Nicola, and brush your teeth and go to sleep."

Back in bed, Nicola lay for a long time with the light on, thinking about Mr. Milton. How his eyes were so blue under his spiky eyebrows. How the things he'd said only *seemed* crazy.

Get them out. Not *him. Them.*

Nicola switched off the light and had a little cry again. In the middle of it, she sat up and turned the light back on.

There it was, where it had been since New Year's Eve, perched on the shade of her bedside lamp. The sign she'd been waiting for, unnoticed all this time.

A little angel-winged blob of wax.

24

___

LATER THAT night it started snowing. Heavy, feathery clumps. It was still snowing the next morning, Saturday, when Nicola walked June Bug to Feeler's Flowers. Over the old snow, dingy with salt and grit and stained with dog pee, a thick white carpet had settled. In front of Feeler's Flowers, under the shelter of the awning, the fresh petals Irene had scattered looked even prettier against this pure new snow.

"Is this June Bug?" Irene called as they came in. "My first dog customer!"

Whenever June Bug found herself in a new place, she had to race around and explore it, sniffing everything in super-snorkel mode.

In the middle of the shop, a reverse sneeze gripped her. *Ork ork ork*, she wheezed. Irene buckled over laughing.

Finally, Nicola managed to distract June Bug with a treat. She made her Sit and Wave and Roll Over.

"She's the cutest dog I've ever seen!" Irene said.

A man in a striped toque with snow stuck in his

beard walked by with a golden Lab. The Lab stopped at the door as though he could read the DOGS WELCOME sign. The man came inside and the two dogs sniffed each other's bottoms to say hello.

"My second dog customer!" Irene said.

"What's your dog's name?" Nicola asked the man.

"Buster."

Irene gave Buster a treat, and June Bug, too. Then the man bought some flowers. "Just because," he said.

"Come back on Valentine's Day, Buster," Nicola said.

After Buster and his owner left, Irene asked how Nicola was feeling.

"Sad," Nicola said. "I was hoping Lindsay would be here."

"She's at home. She won't come out of her box."

"I'll go see her," Nicola said.

"Thank you so much," Irene told Nicola. Then she told June Bug, "Sorry, June Bug, it's a no-pets building."

"I'll take her home first."

"Leave her here," Irene said, even though the little dog was lapping water from a flower bucket on the floor.

"Are you sure?" Nicola asked.

"She's already bringing in customers!"

✳

At the Sheldon Arms Apartments, Nicola met Ignacio shoveling the walk in his big earflapped hat.

"Ah, winter," he told her. "It can put a good janitor to the test. The pipes freezing, the furnace going out. But these little joys, like being the first to walk on freshly fallen snow? They make it all worthwhile. How is June Bug?"

"Good. I left her with Lindsay's mom. She said this was a no-pets building."

Ignacio nodded. "I wish it wasn't, but the owner makes the rules, not me."

"The retirement home I've been visiting with Lindsay and June Bug has a lot of rules. I wonder if Mr. Devon made them or if he's just doing what he's supposed to, like you?"

Ignacio shrugged and continued shoveling.

Nicola stamped her boots on the mat in the lobby, then went up the stairs to Lindsay's apartment. The door was locked. Nicola rang and rang and finally Lindsay, in her pajamas, her glasses all smeary, opened up.

"I *slept* in my box again and I still don't feel better!"

Nicola kicked off her boots. "I got a sign last night."

"What?" Lindsay asked.

"At New Year's we do this special thing in my family." Nicola pulled off her mitts. When she stuffed them in her coat pockets, she dislodged June Bug's treat container. It landed on the floor and the lid popped off. Little heart-shaped salmon treats scattered across the hall.

"Oh," Nicola said, blinking down. "I think we just got another sign."

Lindsay squinted at the treats.

"I thought they glowed to remind us to use our heads," Nicola said. "But that's completely wrong."

Lindsay pushed up her glasses. "They want us to eat dog treats?"

"The shape of them."

Lindsay looked again and broke into a smile. "They want us to use our hearts."

※

Everything made sense then. It was as obvious as the perfect line down the middle of June Bug's half-black, half-white face. June Bug was a good little dog who sometimes did bad things.

They were sitting together on Lindsay's bed.

"Like my dad," she said. "My mom says he's a good man who did something bad."

Then Lindsay crawled into her Feel Better Box and started tearing down the pictures. Glossy magazine brides, Lindsay's own bride drawings, the magazine pictures of happy things — they flew out the end of the box.

Lindsay asked Nicola to pass her the 100 gel pens

that were on her desk. Nicola crawled inside with them. She didn't feel claustrophobic at all.

Good and bad, Lindsay wrote on the wall of the box.

"Love and hate," Nicola said, and Lindsay wrote it down in a different color gel pen. "Life and death."

Tears welled up in Lindsay's eyes, but she wrote it.

"The world is full of opposites," she said.

"We don't like the bad side. Or the hate side. Or the dead side," Nicola said. "But it's there."

"We can stay on the good side if we want," Lindsay said. "If we use our hearts."

✳

On Monday, the most amazing thing happened. Ms. Phibbs brought in a scale and set it up on her desk. Everyone was supposed to guess what combinations of different-sized weights would make the scale balance.

"Lindsay!" Nicola shrieked across the room, for which she had to stay in at recess.

At lunch, the girls couldn't get a seat together in the crowded lunchroom. It was so noisy they wouldn't have been able to talk anyway. They ate their sandwiches separately. Then, as they were leaving, Margo Tamm leapt up from her seat and shoulder-checked Lindsay.

"Look at me! I'm an angel!" She flapped her hands.

Nicola felt like kicking Margo, but Lindsay looked at her with pity.

"I wish you were happier," Lindsay said.

Margo turned red and Lindsay and Nicola walked out together.

They paused to put on their coats in the entrance-way, under the picture of the queen. The kindergarten leaf frieze drooped above it, still covering the school motto.

Nicola looked at the gray-haired queen hanging crookedly. She remembered the kids falling off the playground equipment last fall.

"The world's out of balance," she said.

It had tilted.

With the playground cordoned off, there was nothing to do at recess and lunch. Everyone was bored. Bored, they fought more often.

That day, Gavin Heinrichs chased everyone around, trying to make someone lick the spoon from his lunch that he'd chilled to freezing in a snow bank.

Lindsay and Nicola screamed when he came at them. They ran back into the school and hid in an alcove, but they weren't really safe from Gavin. The school wasn't safe anymore. Or fair, or kind. Ever since Mrs. Dicky fell off the chair last fall, everyone had forgotten the motto. The replacement principal didn't seem to know it, or how to run a school. He didn't know to send the kids in shifts to the lunchroom, or to organize lunch-time activities.

"Remember *Paradise Lost*?" Nicola asked Lindsay.

"How the fallen angels tried to mess people up to get back at the good angels?"

Lindsay stared at Nicola. "Is Gavin a bad angel?"

"No. We don't need fallen angels. We do the messing all by ourselves."

25

At Nicola's house everyone had chores. Jackson, being five, had the easiest. He replaced the toilet paper when it ran out. Because of June Bug, he didn't even need to put it on the roll. He just left it on the windowsill. Nicola set and cleared the table. Jared, unless he forgot or managed to con Nicola into doing it for him, took out the garbage and shoveled the walk.

During dinner that night, Jared argued his case for his own computer. All his friends had one.

"I wish he did, too!" Nicola said.

Mina laughed. "That's nice. You don't usually side with your brother."

"If he had a computer of his own, then I could get on the family computer when I need it."

"You can get on the family computer any time you want," Terence said.

"No," Nicola said. "Last time I had to take out the garbage for him just to check my email."

Terence frowned, which caused Jared to shoot Nicola an evil look.

Jared's annoying behavior annoyed their father. But Terence getting mad, the way he did now, made Nicola feel sorry for her brother. Because of hormones, Jared probably couldn't help being annoying.

"Let me get this straight," Terence told Jared. "You made your little sister do your chore just so she could use the computer, which she has the right to use anyway?"

Head down, Jared shoveled in some casserole.

"And now you'd like me to reward you by buying you your own computer?"

Mina put her hand on Terence's. "Let's just drop it."

"No," Terence said. "I'd like Jared to explain why he should be rewarded for being lazy and selfish."

"Why are you always picking on me?" Jared exploded.

"Because I want you to grow up to be a decent person! You have to do your share around here, young man!"

Jared threw down his fork. His chair scraped across the floor.

After he had stormed from the table, Mina turned to Terence. "That was harsh."

Terence snapped back, "You baby him too much!"

Nicola shrank down. She hated it when her parents argued. Jackson did, too. His bottom lip quivered and he began kicking the leg of the table so that the dishes rattled.

And Nicola blurted, "Everybody around here should just use their hearts a little more!"

In the silence that fell over the table, they could hear Jared smashing something in his room.

"You're right, Nicola," Terence said. "I'll go apologize."

Abruptly, dinner was over. Nicola cleared the table, shuttling back and forth from the dining room to the kitchen with the dirty plates, June Bug at her feet. With Mina occupied getting Jackson into the bath, and Terence having a Talk with Jared, the coast was clear.

Nicola lined up the dishes on the floor. June Bug licked each one clean. Nicola sat on the floor beside her, hugging her knees. She picked up a fork June Bug had scoured with her tongue and spent a minute trying to balance it on one finger.

She thought of something then. When the little dog had finished her chore and Nicola had loaded the dishes in the dishwasher, she went to call Lindsay.

"So there was a big fight here at dinner. My dad said Jared's not doing his share. I think that's why they're not helping each other."

"Who?"

"Mrs. Tanaka, Mr. Fitzpatrick and Mrs. Michaels."

"Huh?"

"It's why they're not just walking out. If angels help each other, nothing's added. They're already one hundred percent pure goodness. But we're not. *We* change the balance, not them. Only the good things we do count."

"So we have to be the angels?"

"I think so. And we have to do what Mr. Milton asked us," Nicola said. "*We* have to get them out."

26

NICOLA AND Lindsay went back to Shady Oaks after school the next day. They kept their eyes open for signs, even watched the Shopping Channel with Mrs. Cream, but couldn't find any significance in the Lint-o-matic Furniture Brush. They walked up and down the shiny halls, allowing June Bug to scratch under Mr. Fitzpatrick's door and, farther down the hall, Mrs. Michaels' and Mrs. Tanaka's.

They tried opening the doors.

Locked.

Nicola pressed her ear against each one. Each time she felt a light vibration.

Glenda appeared, hands on her hips.

"What are you doing?"

Nicola pulled back with a nervous smile. "Could we say hi? June Bug really wants to. Look."

June Bug was crouched down with her nose right in the crack under the door, snorkeling.

"I'd lose my job," Glenda said.

"What if we got in on our own? What if you didn't

know about it? It's mean that they never have visitors."

Glenda waved them out of the hall with broad sweeps of her thin arm. The girls followed her swinging ponytail, disappointed.

When they got to the nursing station, Glenda said goodbye at the same time she pulled a yellow lanyard out of the front pocket of her pajama uniform.

A key hung on the lanyard.

Glenda opened the cupboard where all the medicines were kept. Inside hung two other yellow lanyards with keys. Glenda placed hers on an empty hook.

She turned and said, "Oh," as though she was surprised to see them still standing there watching her. Then, with the cupboard door open and the keys in full view, she buzzed them out, a little smirk brightening her face.

❋

The last sign they needed came on the weekend, on Saturday night, while the Breams were playing rummy.

Jackson dealt first. It was his favorite thing, but his clumsy hands and terrible counting slowed the game. June Bug circled the table pushing an old sock against everyone's legs, trying to get someone to pull it. And Jared did that annoying thing he always did, laying his runs and sets face down on the table instead of face up, so no one knew which cards to stop collecting.

Nicola took hold of the sock. June Bug snarled and tugged on her end, almost pulling Nicola right off her chair.

"June Bug," Mina said. "You're scaring me!"

Triumphantly, Jared laid down another run. He was fiendishly good at cards. Nicola glared at his hoard spreading across the table in front of him. Then she noticed something that made her let go of the sock.

And the funny feeling started up. The fluttery, butterfly feeling she'd been hoping for.

By the time rummy was over, it was too late to call Lindsay.

So it wasn't until Sunday morning that Lindsay got to see the sign. She hurried over to Nicola's house as soon as Nicola called.

Nicola drew the playing card from her back pocket and showed it to Lindsay before she was even out of her coat.

"Three of hearts?" Lindsay said. "Didn't we already get the heart sign?"

Nicola turned over the card and showed Lindsay the pretty curlicued border. Perched in each of the four corners was an angel. But that was not the sign. The sign was in the two circles in the middle of the card, one upside down, one right side up. Two more angels.

Angels on bicycles.

27

———

"WHAT DO YOU think you're doing?" Jared asked on Monday afternoon.

Nicola spun around, as amazed that he was off the computer as she was disappointed to be caught wheeling his BMX toward the basement door.

"I'm borrowing your bike. You're not using it, are you?"

"Duh, it's winter? Or maybe you didn't notice."

"Then you don't need it," Nicola said. "You can borrow something of mine."

"I'm not interested in anything of yours."

This was true. Actually, he wasn't interested in anything except Julie Walters-Chen and playing Inferno 2. And he was probably only interested in Inferno 2 because his own life felt like hell without Julie Walters-Chen. Why this should be, Nicola really, truly didn't understand.

She was supposed to take her own bike and Jared's to Shady Oaks. She'd raced home from school to do it. Lindsay was bringing her bike from the Sheldon Arms Apartments.

Nicola leaned the BMX against the dryer so it made a soft boom like a kettledrum. She folded her hands and took a deep breath.

"If you let me borrow your bike, I'll do something nice for you."

"What?"

"I can't say yet, but I promise you'll be glad you helped me."

"I'm not stupid," Jared huffed. "Show me the goods."

"I can't. But if you help me? If you lend me your bike and carry it to Shady Oaks — "

"Not that place!"

"If you help me there, I think you might be hearing from a certain person."

"Who?"

"Someone with the initials JWC."

Before her eyes, Jared transformed. He grew about four inches and his face reddened enough to camouflage his pimples. Just from mentioning those magic initials.

Then, just as swiftly, he slumped again. "Hearing what?"

"I can't say. But if you ask for help, you'll get it. It might not be exactly what you expect, but it'll still be good. Will you?"

Jared sniffed and scratched his head through his toque.

He mumbled, "Yes," and went and got his coat.

✳

They arrived first. Nicola climbed the fence and opened the back gate for Jared. They set up the two bikes and waited for Lindsay to arrive.

"What are the bikes for?" Jared asked, showing curiosity for the first time.

"You'll see. You're going to be amazed."

"I doubt it."

Finally, Lindsay appeared pushing a bike, pink like her glasses, with a radio hanging off its handlebars and a backpack on her back.

"Jared?" Lindsay said.

Nicola said, "He's going to help. Isn't that great?"

Jared snorted.

The three of them and the dog went around to the front, up the snowy ramp and rang the bell. Jorie buzzed them in.

"It'll have to be a quick visit. I'm leaving in about half an hour."

"Okay," Nicola said. "You remember my brother."

Jorie smiled. Jared twitched.

When Lindsay took the flowers from her backpack, Jorie stepped forward, waving her hands.

"Flowers aren't allowed, sweetie. Remember?"

"I know, but we're not following that rule today. I brought them in memory of Mr. Milton," Lindsay told her.

Jorie's eyes brimmed up. "Okay. I'll take them home with me when I leave. Let me find something to put them in. Go ahead to the lounge. They're all there."

"Could you bring a bowl, too?" Lindsay asked. "For the potato chips."

"Potato chips?" Jorie squeaked. She glanced nervously around, then whispered, "Mr. Devon's in his office."

The girls exchanged a wide-eyed look.

In the lounge Mr. Eagleton was already sitting at the table staring at nothing. Nicola pulled out the chair next to him. June Bug jumped up and wagged at Mr. Eagleton, who turned his head with underwater slowness and looked at the dog and smiled.

Nicola told Jared to bring Mrs. Cream over. She wheeled Miss Higgins.

Meanwhile, Lindsay turned off the TV.

All at once they could hear it, the faint wine-glass ringing they'd heard the day June Bug put on her show for everybody.

The first amazing thing happened then, though Jared didn't realize it. He sat at the table with the others, his toque pulled low over his eyes, breathing through his mouth, unaware that Miss Higgins had never in any of their visits so much as lifted her chin off her chest.

She did now. The ringing had woken her. First her head, covered in fine white hair, floated up like a dandelion gone to seed. Then her eyes opened. They were hazel and circled with silver.

"What's that?" she asked.

Jorie was just coming back with a pitcher filled with water and a plastic mixing bowl for the chips. She stopped.

"Miss Higgins? Did you say something?"

"I asked about that sound. I hear it now and then. It's louder now."

"It's the other patients," Jorie said. "They hum. Isn't it lovely? But, Miss Higgins? I'm quite flabbergasted that you're talking like this."

Nicola took the pack of cards out of her pocket and asked Jared to shuffle. Then she headed for the nursing station. She didn't look back to see if Jorie was watching. She simply walked behind the desk, opened the cupboard and took what she needed.

When she did look back, Jorie was arranging Lindsay's flowers. June Bug was sitting with everyone at the table Waving her paw, hoping for one of the potato chips Lindsay was pouring into the bowl.

Nicola skated as fast as she could in her socks down the slippery hall to Mr. Fitzpatrick's room. She had just slid the key in the lock when someone at the far end of the hall called out.

"What do you think you're doing?"

A cold feeling washed over Nicola, a clammy feeling, like just before you throw up. She hated that feeling, knowing when it was over you'd feel so much better, but still dreading what was going to happen.

Slowly, she turned her head.

There was Mr. Devon in his black suit and smoky glasses, striding toward her, the odor of cigarette smoke growing stronger, competing with the flowery smell. Strangely, though, he seemed to become smaller and more ordinary as he drew near.

Then he was standing in front of her, not a big hulking creature with horns, just a man. He was shorter than her father, his face sour and pinched. His eyes, as far as she could see through the tinted lenses of his glasses, weren't red, but brown.

"You heard me," he said in a nasal voice. "What do you think you're doing?"

"We're having a party. Everyone's invited. Even you."

"A party?"

"I know," Nicola said. "Parties aren't allowed. Why do you have so many awful rules?"

"I don't make them. I'm only running the place. And on a very tight budget. There's no money for parties."

"Okay. But why can't people bring flowers? Or food?"

"Like I said, my employer's in charge."

"Why is Mr. Fitzpatrick locked in?" Nicola asked. "And Mrs. Michaels and Mrs. Tanaka?"

"You'll have to take that question to my employer. Now— "

"Who *is* your employer, Mr. Devon?" Nicola asked.

Mr. Devon seemed to freeze for a moment. Then he exploded.

"Leave! All of you!"

Nicola pushed Mr. Fitzpatrick's door wide open. Mr. Devon scrambled to close it, allowing Nicola to skate ahead, unlock and fling open Mrs. Michaels' door. Mr. Devon rushed to close that one, too. By then Nicola had opened Mrs. Tanaka's door.

She burst past Mr. Devon, calling behind her, "Come to the party! Everyone's invited!"

In the lounge, Jared was dealing cards while Jorie hovered, wringing her chapped hands.

"There's a rule against games," she said.

Nicola slipped onto her chair beside June Bug. Mr. Eagleton looked down at the two angels on bicycles on the cards that landed in front of him. He smiled in slow motion.

"What's that smell?" Miss Higgins asked.

"It's the flowers, dear." Jorie pointed to the bouquet in the middle of the table, between the chips and the radio. "Aren't they beautiful?"

"It's not the flowers," Nicola said. "It's the other patients."

Jorie stared and pressed her heart.

"Play with us, Jorie," Lindsay begged. "It'll be fun. I'll put on some music."

"Music!" Jorie yelped. She sank onto a chair, looking dazed. "Mr. Devon will be here any second."

"He's on his way," Nicola said.

Maybe the amazing thing that happened next wouldn't have happened if Lindsay hadn't turned on the Golden Oldies station. Maybe if a different old song had come on the radio. Maybe if the old people and Jorie, who all knew the words to the song, too, hadn't started singing. But that was impossible because it was one of those catchy songs impossible not to sing along to.

The song was about a teenaged girl killed in a tragic car accident. Her boyfriend was calling out to her, calling her an angel.

Everyone started singing the angel chorus, even Mr. Eagleton.

Jared was still unamazed. He didn't know that Mr. Eagleton barely spoke and that Mrs. Cream's vocabulary normally consisted of a single nonsense word. He mimed a finger down his throat to show how he felt about the song, though a second later even his lips were moving with the words.

"Jorie!" came a booming, nasal voice. Jorie started fanning her face wildly with her cards even as she was singing "Teen Angel" with the others.

Black-suited Mr. Devon bore down on the table.

Singing! Music! Potato chips! Games!

"Where are the keys, Jorie?" he roared. "They aren't in the cupboard."

Jorie looked up at him in terror and bewilderment.

Jared was unamazed by the sudden appearance of Mr. Devon. He didn't know about the manager of Shady Oaks. He went right on playing, asking Miss Higgins, "What's your name again?"

"Higgins."

"Okay. Miss Higgins? Your deal. Should I shuffle for you?"

"That would be lovely."

Mr. Devon reached out and snapped off the radio, but the old dears went on singing. Singing about angels and true love. Lindsay giggled nervously.

Mr. Devon slammed his fist on the table. "No laughing!"

"Whoa," Jared said, shuffling. "What's your problem?"

With a crabbed hand, Miss Higgins accepted the deck of cards Jared slid over to her. "It's getting louder."

She meant the wine-glass hum. When Mr. Devon realized it, he swung around.

June Bug, whose hearing and sense of smell were so much more powerful, had already jumped off her chair. She was creeping toward the hall.

Nicola and Lindsay went after the dog. Jorie and Mr. Devon followed.

Jared called, "Are we playing or not?" Then he got up, too.

Three doors stood open. Three fragile figures had emerged and were wriggling inside their too-large robes like caterpillars struggling in their cocoons. The hall vibrated with their clear, high ringing. The beautiful scent of flowers filled the air.

June Bug's ears flattened against her head. She cast her black eyes down and curtsied.

Tiny Mrs. Michaels' pink robe fell around her feet first. Next Mr. Fitzpatrick freed himself of his. Then Mrs. Tanaka.

The hunch on their backs was wings. Wings that began to unfold like pairs of gauzy sails.

By then the hall had filled with a strange light. It radiated off the three sets of wings unfurling and stretching out, rippling colors, an aurora borealis strobing across the walls.

And then there were no wings. Only light.

All of this Jared saw and, like his sister and her friend Lindsay and her dog, like Jorie and maybe even Mr. Devon, the most beautiful, peaceful feeling came over him.

He was amazed.

28

—

WHAT MUST HAVE happened was this.

The whole neighborhood — Nicola's house and the Sheldon Arms Apartments, Feeler's Flowers, Shady Oaks Retirement Home and Queen Elizabeth Elementary School —

s t r a i g h t e n e d.

Tuesday, the day after the angels escaped, the picture of the queen in the front entrance of Queen Elizabeth Elementary was hanging properly on its nail, the crown perched evenly on Her Majesty's head.

Everyone felt it. The kids milling in the schoolyard at recess could even *see* it. On the other side of the yellow caution tape, the playground equipment stood on level ground.

At first only Nicola Bream and Lindsay Feeler dared to duck under the tape. They were less nervous about breaking rules, having recently had so much practice at it. They felt like zoo animals, stared at from the outside as they swung wildly on the swings.

One by one, the others slipped under and joined them. All except Gavin Heinrichs, who flung himself at the tape like a runner crossing the finish line, and broke it.

The girls might have got in trouble, except this happened the very day Mrs. Dicky returned from her sick leave. Appalled that nothing had been done about the equipment while she was away, she called the school board. The inspector came, and the next day confirmed what they knew anyway. The playground was perfectly safe.

Something else was different, too. The birds returned. It really seemed that one day there were none and the next, on every branch you saw a cheery cardinal or a twittering waxwing. They arranged themselves like red and yellow decorations, singing out their hearts.

The birds returned because of the change in the weather, or so everyone said. Finally, the cold snap broke and overnight the temperature rose enough that hats and scarves no longer seemed a matter of life or death. This gave everyone hope that one day the snow would melt and the earth would come alive again, like it did every year. The snowdrops and crocuses would nudge their noses out of the earth, and spring would come bursting in.

"Listen to this," Terence said on Saturday morning while he and Mina sat at the table drinking coffee, Mina working on the crossword puzzle, Terence reading the paper.

"The practice of sedating troublesome elderly patients in care facilities has become common in the region."

"What's sedating?" Nicola asked from where she sat on the floor eating cereal with June Bug. One spoon for Nicola, one for June Bug. Her parents wouldn't notice. They loved the weekend paper.

"Giving sleeping medication," Mina answered.

"The government has started a task force to look into the practice, which is called snowing."

"Snowing?" Nicola said. And she shivered.

Mina looked up from her puzzle. "Oh, Nicola! Weren't you telling me something about that?"

※

To: Nicola Bream and Lindsay Feeler
From: Patient Quality Care Office

Dear Ms. Bream and Ms. Feeler,
Thank you for your letter concerning Shady Oaks Retirement Home. I am writing to inform you that Shady Oaks was recently closed due to the overwhelming number of complaints we received from staff and visitors to the facility. Numerous health violations were of special concern. Please be assured that

the remaining patients have been resettled and are now receiving excellent care.

Nicola and Lindsay took this letter as a good sign. But not everything was a sign. They'd figured that out walking the bicycles home from Shady Oaks that amazing afternoon.

The bicycles had turned out not to be needed.

Because who needs wheels when you have wings?

✳

The following Monday, Ms. Phibbs opened her desk drawer and found it completely stuffed with flower petals.

A silence fell over the class. There was only one person who could get hold of that many flower petals in winter. Still, breath held, they all watched to see what Ms. Phibbs would do next.

Ms. Phibbs bowed forward until her forehead touched her desk. Her shoulders began to shake. Nicola thought she must be crying. When she straightened, there were even tears in her eyes.

She was laughing.

Ms. Phibbs wiped her face with a tissue she pulled from her sleeve.

"I believe Mrs. Dicky arranged to have the gymnastics equipment set up. Please, everybody. Put on your gym shoes."